Once and Future

Tales of Eirlandia Book One

MARICLAIRE NORTON

Title: Once and Future

Subtitle: Tales of Eirlandia, Book One

Author: Mariclaire Norton

Cover Art: Seerendip Publishing

Publisher: Seerendip Publishing

Edition: First printing, 2025

ISBN: 978-1-965273-14-2 (Paperback)

Library of Congress Control Number: 2025907903

Printed in the United States of America

*Dedicated to my most wonderful husband and
muse and the Alaric to my Tara.*

Prologue

MAEVE

When Maeve entered the old, dusty library, she could feel the weight of the centuries in the air. She would have loved to have the time to explore this wondrous place fully, but she knew that time was short. She took a deep breath, breathing in the smell of old parchment, wood and stone. Heaving a great sigh, she shook herself and thought about the tremendous task she had set out to do.

She had left her cloak and horse at her campsite, which was over a day's travel away. She had not wanted anything to give the location of the library away. Her cloak would be a dead giveaway of what she was, a member of the renown warrior class known as the Fighdrui. Her clan, for want of a better word, was charged with guarding the most important of the government figures, and she herself was the chief of the personal bodyguard of the ArdRighian. She was sometimes assigned ancillary duties, such as this one, which required a personal knowledge of the ancient histories and the mage powers to deal with the spells and possible traps of this ancient library. She was unconcerned about her horse, as the Keepers of the waystation would take care of it.

Maeve was proud of who she was, a strong and fearless warrior, a sometimes spy, a minor mage and, if she was honest, a good-looking woman. Her dark red hair was cut in an old pageboy style, but it suited her. Her eyes were an unusual color, almost a grey, but they could change to a light blue or green depending on what she wore and the colors around her. She'd been told by many a young date that she had an almost other-worldly look about her, as if she was something more than just Eirlandian. Maeve always shrugged, she didn't know much about her parentage or heritage, and never cared to learn. It just wasn't important to her. What was important, at that moment, was finding Tara Prima's journal and the knowledge it contained.

Although the former ArdRighian Tara Prima and her consort, King Alaric, were only the stuff of legends to the general public, Maeve knew from her studies as a Fighdrui that they had indeed lived. That meant the lost Journal of the ArdRighian Tara Prima, was in here someplace. "I hope Tara Prima wrote a good journal," she said softly. She recalled all the legends and history of the famous pair. Tara's life from minor nobility to the wife of the prince of Vikland and, later, ArdRighian of Eirlandia, was required learning for all Fighdrui. Most people knew only the legends that had grown up around the pair in the centuries since their death, but the Drui class, which included the Fighdrui, were taught the truth behind legends. Tara Prima's deeds once saved Eirlandia from conquest, but now the time had come again when her legacy would be required to again defend against their ancient enemy. The enormity of her mission threatened to overwhelm her, and Maeve clapped her hands together to stop the feelings. 'This is not the time to panic,' she told herself. 'Tara Secunda is counting on you. Get a grip, Lass!'

"Okay," she muttered to herself, "time to find the hiding place."

With a slight thrust to the tote on her back, she turned on the all-light. The sudden illumination of the dark interior brought a grim smile to her face. She remembered what she had been told about the location of the Journal. "The signs would be there for those who know the way." So Aelfund, the leader of the Fighdrui and her supervisor had told her when explaining her mission. "Remember your training, Maeve, and look for what is hidden in plain sight. Your knowledge of High Eirl will stand you in good stead."

The library fell within the territory of the Rebel Righs. These minor tribal kings had been a thorn in side of the government since Tara Prima's time. They still refused to give up their squabbles over territory and to pay their full taxes, even though the government was no longer a monarchy but a republic. Having disguised her passage to her destination, she had successfully skirted any chance of encounter with the ferocious brigands. This, she reckoned, gave her plenty of time to find the Book of Tara and leave a different way, without incident.

Leaving the all-light in its place, she started forward. Smaller lights would show her the way once she got beyond the main room. For now, it was bright enough to read the signs pointing to the various vaults leading off from the main chamber.

Since she had found the library sealed upon her arrival, she could be sure nothing lived inside these huge walls. She had easily figured out the magic behind the seal. Her training in High Eirl and mage-craft assured that she would be able to pass any tests easily. The years she had spent becoming a Fighdrui had been filled with challenges, but Maeve knew the hours, days and even months learning the ancient language, and the histories and spells of her craft, were worth it.

She ventured ahead, remembering the words of the ArdDrui before leaving Kilawey.

"The Great Library was destroyed just after the deaths of Tara and Alaric," Elaroth had told Maeve. "The ArdDrui of the time, Culluchan, sealed the vault and concealed its location so that the warring factions could not find the book. When the armies invaded the library, where they knew the book was hidden, and could not locate the chamber, they took their frustration out on the rest of the building. Many important works were lost because of their anger and destruction.

"The rebel Righs did not find the vault because it was hidden in plain sight," Elaroth had continued. "The ArdDrui wanted to make sure only the authorized would be allowed to actually find and return the book. That was another surety placed, so that the book would not fall into the wrong hands. Each new ArdDrui is told the location of the vault at their investiture, but only a Fighdrui is authorized to retrieve the journal, and only a Fighdrui is told how to find the spot within the library.

"Be careful, be cautious, but you should come to no harm in that place; at least not from the library itself. Follow my instructions and look for the vault's opening. There the book stands open for all to read, yet the pages cannot be moved."

As a Fighdrui, Maeve knew more than the average Eirlandian regarding the true history of her country. She was also aware that if she could safely return with her find to Kilawey, she could help bring back peace to her land. The old enemies were once again stirring, and all records pointed to Tara Prima's journal as the key to finding the magical items that would be necessary to finally completely overcome their ancient enemy.

"Spirit of Tara Prima, be with me," she whispered softly. "Help me find that which was hidden so that this land will continue as it should and not be overwhelmed by those who mean it and its people harm."

Like stone chimneys, the books rose on all sides. Cautiously, she weaved through overturned shelves. She climbed over the piles when she could not go around, sorry for every footfall that caused even more destruction to the pages beneath her, but there was nothing she could do about that. As she threaded her way through the stacks, she breathed through her mouth, so as to not start a sneezing fit because of the dust. Her shoes left a clear sign of her passage, but she was sure no one had followed, so she was not concerned.

About halfway down the main aisle, she noticed a sigil placed on the floor. To one not trained in High Eirl, it looked little more than a decoration. But the design was much more than that; it indicated a direction.

"Down this way lies the path to the past," the sigil read. "Do not let appearances deceive, for while all may gaze, only few can read."

Reading that, Maeve smiled slightly. Taking a smaller all-light, she proceeded down the smaller aisle that led off from the main corridor. Sweeping the light left and right, she shortly came to what appeared as the end of the passageway. She saw a small alcove before her containing a statue of a large book, opened to a page square in the middle.

The words were High Eirl. Like the sigil, they would have been unreadable except to a few at the time of installation and even fewer in this time.

Following the instructions on the book, Maeve spoke the words. Slowly the massive book moved, and a small doorway appeared where it had been solid wall. Taking the light with her, Maeve moved slowly into the hole, unsure of what she would find.

The corridor was not long, and she soon found herself in a small but well-appointed chamber. A few tables and chairs were strewn about. Old all-lights lined the walls.

The large display case in the center of the room caught her attention. Walking closer, she realized it was made of almonite, a rare mineral used to protect extremely fragile and precious objects. Almost impossible to break and extremely costly, only the ruling class could afford it and they did so on rare occasions.

Almonite had been perfected by a master magician who lived a hundred years before Tara Prima. She had created the mineral using alchemic formulas now lost to history, but it was well known the mineral could absorb magic well. To create an enclosure of this size from it required magic during its construction. It told Maeve she had found what she sought.

Stepping even closer, she took in the neat handwriting revealed in the open page. She scanned the pages revealed, wondering to herself why the ArdDrui had chosen to have the book open instead of closed. But pages spoke only of general occurrences that were well documented in government papers, and hardly secret. She knew she was the first to see this priceless treasure in centuries.

There was no latch to the case. Magic sealed it. Maeve noted with amazement that no trace of dust lay on the case. In contrast, her tan, form-fitting tunic and leggings were several shades lighter than normal because of the dust. Pausing a moment, she ran a hand through her hair, stirring the dust that had settled on her locks.

"Okay, Lass," she said to herself. "First things first, let's get that book." Already provided with the opening spell, she put down her pack on a desk and approached the book.

Before she did anything else, she spoke the words to turn on the all-lights dotting the walls. Burning dimly, they soon grew to a good glow.

Since it had been the personal journal of the ArdRighian, the Journal of Tara Prima was an easy size to handle. The cover gave an impression of being leather, although Maeve could tell it was something stronger than hide. It showed no signs of age or disintegration.

Using her hands to create the appropriate pattern, she spoke the opening spell in High Eirl. "Open this box, that I might claim that which is mine by right," she intoned. "By the power of the Fighdrui, I summon the author of this book to hear me and grant me this request."

The material surrounding the book glowed for a moment then the almonite covering parted into two halves and slid down onto the table on which it stood. The Book stood open to the air for the first time in centuries. Curiously, during that few seconds when the case had glowed, the book had somehow closed, and the cover, which was of a dark blue leather, was adorned only with the words "Tara's Journal."

Maeve stood in reverent silence for a few moments, remembering her lessons regarding this document. It was said there was an ancient prophecy that spoke of a queen and her foreign king who would use unique magic to create crowns that would ensure the peace and prosperity of Eirlandia after a great battle. This ArdRighian would have in her possession a wondrous magical stone, the Lifenstone, which would be a legacy from her Sidheran mother. With this stone she would have the power to defeat the Formorrid, their ancient enemy. But although the great work would last many generations, there would come a time when the enemy would arise again and the Lifenstone and Ruling Crowns would again be needed.

That time had come, and Maeve's task was to recover, and bring back, the journal of ArdRighian Tara Prima, which was believed to hold the location of the Master Lifenstone and the Ruling Crowns. Taking a deep breath, Maeve sent a silent plea to the Old Ones that she would be granted the opportunity to be a part of the recovery process of these precious artifacts.

With wide eyes and gentle hands, Maeve lifted the journal from its resting place and placed it on a nearby table. Reverently she turned back the cover and began to read.

Chapter 1

TARA

My mistakes shape my story, much like my successes. You, whose days lie far in the future, will see that mistakes are peerless teachers. For those of us whose lot ever included the rule of a kingdom, we must soon acknowledge the nonpareil dangers of our position even though it bore us certain coveted dispensations.

This journal is my story. Much has been written about me, but these are my personal thoughts. As such, I shall begin at a time when I was princess of a minor kingdom in Eirlandia. My father was a lesser Righ who worried about his people more than it was considered normal for his day.

Never bred to have a taste for war, Righ Eduar often saw raids by the Vikes. His army had never been as large or as strong as those harbored by other small kingdoms surrounding us.

Not fertile land or trade goods, but sheep and cattle accounted for our wealth. Even though fairly poor, our kingdom traded with others in peace. No one chose to permanently invade us.

The Vikes, however, raided us for our animals. They fed them to their crews during the raids, selling the hides to their own people upon return to their land. Our animals were prized for skins which could be worked into many useful commodities.

It was a soft spring day. Outside the early spring air held a touch of morning fog. I would have much rather been outside, but since my father and older brother were away on a diplomatic mission, I surrogated the duties of Righ Eduar.

The daylight cascaded gently into the chamber, illuminating the tapestries that hung on the wall. This was a minor court in one of the larger towns within our Tuath. Glin was a port town, but was far from the normal raiding routes of the Viks, since its waterways did not meet up with any outlet to the sea. Therefore, my father and brother decided to move court temporarily to Glin while they were away, in order to minimize the risk of a possible raid in their absence.

I was in the midst of figuring out the implications of a boundary dispute between two husbandmen, when one of the guards bolted in through the doors.

One look at his bloodied face and ripped tunic told me there was serious trouble. The royal Fighdrui guards were better trained than to come running in during an audience session.

"Raiders," he shouted. "Raiders in the town! Run, my Lady, hide! They're taking slaves."

Confusion spread through the hall immediately. Standing up, I stepped off the dais and held out my hand to stop his advance. "The Vikes never capture slaves in Glin," I said to the panting guard.

"They've already rounded up a dozen!" he answered. "Only women, mostly of your age. You must go. You're the ruler in the absence of your father and brother. Go. Now! Use the tunnels."

I will admit it was a fine day for raiding a port town like Glin. Our harbor on the Shenon was small but with enough draft to let in a warship. How come there was no warning of the approaching ship? Advance raiders reaching the watchmen at their posts, killing or knocking them out, thus stifling any chance of an alarm being sounded could be the only explanation.

In seconds after the guard's warning, I was running down the hall, shouting for my maid to gather clothes and food before meeting me at the entrance to the tunnels. The tumult and confusion told me I would probably not hear the maid's reply.

No sooner had I reached the mouth of the tunnels than I was greeted by a Vike warrior. It was at that moment I realized my maid was not coming.

Taller than most Eirlandians, and I suspected most Vikes, the man stood in full battle dress, patiently awaiting my arrival. His long brown hair was braided, his strong arms and legs visible through the short tunic he wore. His eyes were also a dark brown, but his face, to my surprise, was mostly clean shaven, except for a long, braided goatee.

"So, the little eaglet tries to fly away," he growled in Eirl, surprising me. "Good thing I was told about this back door; or we'd have lost our main prize."

I swiftly turned as he started toward me but another Vike blocked my advance. Younger than the first one, his braided blond hair did not grow as long. A face thoroughly shaven, his mail boasted finer and richer material, making me wonder if he was superior to his mate.

His blue-grey eyes twinkled with the glee of watching me trapped.

It's a game to them, I thought, bile surging within me. They'll soon find out how serious this game can get. I might be a noble, but I knew how to defend myself.

Seeing no way around them, I was taken aback. But I reached down in a flash and drew my dagger. They couldn't take me without a fight.

The younger Vike hooted: "Oh, no. The eaglet has talons." He took a casual step toward me. "I'd like to see an Eirlandian woman display her combat skills."

Seeing I made no move, he taunted me: "Come on, eaglet, or are you really only a dove in disguise?"

Even a child could see I wasn't dressed for a fight. I still wore a long, encumbering skirt, not just trews, which was my garb of choice. Still, I took a stance and waited as the Vike slowly approached me. It was a relief he didn't draw his sword. But I was somewhat insulted when he didn't go for his dagger either. It appeared he believed he would get the best of me even though he was weaponless.

"You may find me harder to subdue than you think." My voice was soft yet firm. I felt another presence inside my mind, one that seemed to know exactly what was going to happen. Could he see it in my eyes? I had never experienced this feeling before, but I embraced the sensation. Hearing tales of such things by members of the Fighdrui who served in my father's guard, I knew that of which they spoke. I had simply never been in a situation where I felt I was in real danger, so the 'Morrigan Mind', as this feeling was called, had never occurred to me.

With my free hand, I reached around me and undid the clasp to my overdress. It spilled as I stepped out of the encumbering skirt.

My tunic and trews always stayed under my skirts. Although my father wasn't warlike, he made sure I knew how to defend myself. I could have chanced upon a brigand anytime during one of my excursions on horseback. Nothing made me compromise my love of riding and indulging my freedom. So, Eduar had seen to it that I was trained alongside my brother. I knew how to throw someone larger and heavier than myself off balance.

The first Vike chuckled. "Looks like your eaglet came prepared, Alaric," he said to the second man. They spoke again in my language. "You had best watch out. I hear some of these women are decent fighters."

Alaric growled back in Vik. "No woman born can best me." His pushed his tongue along his cheek, licking the corner of his mouth when he added, "But I'll be careful, Sven. I don't want to damage the merchandise."

He suddenly leapt toward me and all became a blur.

I dodged the charge, hitting his back with the hilt of my dagger as he dashed past. Whirling, I feigned a swipe at his face and got some space between us. The older Vike simply kept out of our way, watching intently. Alaric recovered from his failed attempt, quickly turned, grabbed at my wrist, and missed.

A faint growl under his breath, he came at me low and stood upright all at once. His foot swept under mine, knocking me off balance. As I went down, I tried to roll away but the chamber was too small. Hard against one wall, out of room to maneuver, I found myself looking up at Alaric as he stood over me. I didn't know what these men wanted, but I assumed slaves. I decided I would declare who I was, and bargain for ransom, which I am sure my father would pay.

Prudently out of reach of the dagger I held, he grinned. "Not bad, little eagle," he commented, shifting back to Eirl, "If the room had been bigger, no doubt you'd have gone on several minutes further before I got you." My chest heaving with breath at being mocked, he went on, "You are mine now by right of conquest. You can come quietly and with dignity or you can try to fight, in which case I shall disarm you, tie you up and haul you out of here over my shoulder. Which shall it be?"

I glared at this arrogant Vike with malice.

"I am of royal blood." My tone was quiet, but I made sure he heard me clearly. "I will not be manhandled by anyone for any reason. I will come quietly and with dignity. But I give no promise of not trying to escape if the opportunity arises. You are not Eirlandian, you do not deserve my respect."

Alaric looked at me with his hard, grey eyes. "So be it, BanRigh. In this land you outrank me. Not that it matters. You may be ruler here, but not where you're going with me."

"I am not BanRigh," I protested. "My father is Righ and my brother Tanist before me. I'm in line should anything happen to them, but I'm not…" The words died on my tongue as I looked up into eyes that had suddenly grown soft and cloudy. His face became gentle and almost sorrowful.

"Your father and brother are dead, Tanista Tara" he said reluctantly. "They were killed yesterday in a raid by other Vikes not allied with me. We're getting out of here before any of your people find out and raise the army to your aid. You are BanRigh by right of blood, but you'll never rule here." With that, he took my arm and pulled me up to him.

My nerveless fingers did not resist when he took my dagger. Father! Elmond! The echoes swirled through my head. I felt tears begin to form, but I blinked them away, I would not show weakness before these men! But my heart ached, nonetheless.

"Dead?" My voice hardly trickled forth from my lips.

"Dead," he agreed. My eyes wandered down his front and over to the floor. "Whatever's left of their escort is making its way back here with the bodies as we speak," his fingers closed around my elbow, "we are taking ship with the tide so we're well away before they can do anything."

Picking up my overdress, he handed it to Sven and addressed him. "Send men to find other garments of that size and type. Right now we need to get the Tanista and ourselves out of here. Go through the back chamber door, make sure it's clear."

Sven nodded and opened the back door that led under the walls of the town and out to the dock. Alaric looked at me, and said, "Do not resist, Tanista, it will be easier if you just let me do what I must. With that, Alaric turned me around, gagged me and threw a piece of cloth over my head.

"I cannot risk you getting loose," he told me, binding my wrists behind me. "No one will see you or, if they do, know who you are in those trews and hood. The gag will keep you from crying out. I will release you once we are on my ship and away from Glin."

He promptly hauled me up and over his shoulder, then he went down the tunnel and, after what seemed like a long time, up the walkway to his ship.

During this time I could only hear, and for the most part he must have kept to back ways, for at no time did I hear voices raised in question or protest of what must have been a strange sight. I could only smell the sea, and I think the cloth might have held fish at some point, as the smell was strong and masked whatever other odors might have been around that could have told me where we were and even where we were headed.

Instead I spent the time thinking about my father and brother, letting the tears flow now, since there was no one to see me. I was frightened, I admit. While one heard stories about the Vikes and their raid, I never believed myself to be in danger. I wondered if what I had been told was true about them, but realized he would have no reason to lie. Obviously my capture was made on purpose, as this Alaric clearly knew who I was. I could not, however, begin to think of a reason why I would be kidnapped. My family's tuath was not large or particularly important. Although well off, my father was hardly the richest of the tribal kings. Any ransom would be decent, but not enough to go through all this trouble. And if my father and brother were dead, who would they go for the ransom? The chieftains would not necessarily want to bother with ransoming me. I was not Tanista, I would have soon been married off to some other Righ's Tanist I am sure, but the council would look for a male heir first before they would consider me. All these thoughts, and more, ran through my head until it ached.

I realized from the sudden upward slope that we had reached the ship. Once onboard, Alaric handed me over to someone else who took me to a room and sat me down. He did not speak to me, but I heard his voice softly speaking to others, so I knew he was male. He made me comfortable, sitting me on a cushioned chair, but did not remove my hood or bonds. From my seat I heard the sounds of the ship weighing anchor, and felt her pulling away from the dock. I waited in silence, not sure if my guard was still there or not, as I had not heard the door open and close again.

It was some time before I heard the door open again. "My Prince," I heard a man say. Just then the cloth was removed, along with my bounds and gag.

Alaric stood there, cleaned up and finally looking like the prince someone had just named him.

"Well, Tanista, I hope your wait wasn't too bad," he said in a mocking voice. "We're well away from Glin, and will be stopping along the coast sometime tomorrow for a little while before we head to Vikland." He smiled as he declared that, obviously hoping to look less formidable.

I said nothing, so he continued, although his smile slipped a bit. "I assume you wish to freshen up and then take some food and drink?" he asked. I nodded in silence.

"There's nowhere you can escape from here. You may have the run of the ship, except the cargo holds. You will have a personal guard, as some of my men don't understand that you're not to be touched by anyone. Your guard will also be your guide and will get you anything you need. Do not set foot outside this cabin without Vilk."

He gestured to a small, young man standing by the door. I assumed he had been the person with me before Alaric arrived. "Vilk may look small and young, but he's a seasoned warrior. My men respect him. He'll be your constant companion unless I am with you. Is that clear?"

Although Alaric spoke in a mild voice, his intent was clear. I was a prisoner, albeit an important one. I would be guarded carefully.

A small voice inside my head seemed to answer his question. I remember speaking the words, "I understand," and watching Alaric leave. But most of me was, I think now, in shock. I was numb from learning that I was orphaned, and would likely never see my homeland again, much less attend my father and brother's funeral. One thing I did understand, until we reached a harbor again, there was little I could do. I felt sure there would be time to catch him off-guard. I was a good swimmer. Assuming they kept close enough to a shore, I could dive and reach land before they had a chance to recapture me. The Vikes could not keep me captive for long! The practical side of me realized that playing the cowed captive was my best course of action right now. There would be time later to properly mourn my losses and plot my escape.

I will admit that Vilk was not the rough and tumble guard I expected. While he watched me closely, he obviously was trying to be helpful and unobtrusive. I realized he didn't look like a typical Vike. Slight of build with brown eyes and hair, his skin wasn't so much tanned as a slightly brownish color that seemed his natural coloring.

The rest of the day I sifted through the clothes Alaric's men had brought aboard. Most of them fit, although only a few were actually mine. Some clothes were completely different than what I was used to and I assumed they were Vike clothes. Down they went to the bottom of the chest because with luck I might never need them. The fancier dresses sat on top of the foreign clothes. I made sure workday clothing and night wear were visible as soon as I swung open the steamer's lid. Besides I would need the pairs of shoes, trews and hose.

I picked out a new pair of trews and blouse and skirt that matched. I could use the wide belt I had on easily enough, and the boots would be more practical than the indoor shoes I now wore. Stepping to a small screened area, I changed quickly, then put the clothes I had been wearing into an empty hamper, which I assumed was to be used for dirty clothes.

Once all was arranged to my satisfaction, I asked Vilk if we could go topside for some fresh air. He nodded and gestured me out before him.

"Be careful on the stairs, my lady." Vilk's voice was low pitched for one so seemingly young. It took me a moment to realize he had spoken in Eirl, not Vike. "The stairs are sometimes slippery. Some of the men like to play tricks on captives and will wax the stairs coming up from your chambers in the hopes the captive will slip and fall." He smiled up at me, "the men get bored easily, you see."

"Thank you for the warning," I replied in my own tongue as I continued up the stairs.

It appeared the crew had not tried the wax trick, for the stairs were steep but solid underfoot.

Once topside I went immediately to the rail, but saw only sea and a small smear on the horizon that could have been land. Before taking my next breath, Alaric was beside me.

"That's the coast." he said, as if reading my thoughts. "But we have a way to go before we land again. We're putting out beyond the range of your people's pursuit boats. Supper's ready. I was about to come get you from your cabin."

He took my arm gently and escorted me down a stairway to the eating area. "I don't usually eat with the crew" he told me on the way, "but I want to formally introduce you and let everyone know they can't trifle with you in any way."

At the bottom of the stairs, he stepped before me and walked down a short corridor before opening a door.

The smell of unwashed bodies mixed with food overpowered me. Alaric was clean, so was Vilk. Even the older Vike I had heard referred to as Sven threw no horrible odor. But dirt, salt, mead, whiskey, and the gods only knew what else wafted up from the crew, mixing with the stench with that of onion and fish. I coughed and my eyes watered. Alaric looked back at me sharply, and I blinked and swallowed. I would not have his men see me weak in any way. Seeing my reaction to his look, he smiled thinly. He seemed to know what I was thinking and approved.

He stood in the doorway for a moment watching the noisy crowd. Soon, silence descended inside the large eating room. Even the cook stopped in his tracks to look at the young Vike.

Then a rumble replaced the calm. "Al-ar-ic, Al-ar-ic!" the men chanted. "Alaric, Alaric, Alaric, Vike, Vike, Vike!" they continued, shouting louder. After several seconds Alaric put up his hand and everyone was quiet again.

"Good crew! My brave men, my hearty Vikes, I give you greetings and bless you in the name of the All-Father as your prince. We came away today with much loot, several slaves, and a very special prize, a Tanista of Eirlandian blood. Our raid was a great success, and my father will be well pleased with all of you. The All-Father Woodooen has surely blessed us and you will share in all the spoils, but one."

As he said this, he reached behind him and grabbed my arm, pulling me around and in front of him.

"This is the spoil you may not have. This is Tanista Tara, former princess of the Eirlandians and destined to be BanRigh of her tribe. Now she is mine and will not be a BanRigh of the Eirlandians, but Truwif to me, Alaric, son of King Leeife of the Vike! Look upon her and remember her. Treat her with respect when you see her and do not assume her helpless if you see her alone. If she is harmed in any way by any one of you, that one shall swiftly meet Woodooen in his moon house and not as a warrior. Understood?"

During his little speech, my mind and emotions were in a whirl. I knew enough Vik to know what a Truwif was, a wife, usually the head wife, as it was said some Vikes had multiple wives. I felt myself tense up. If this man, this prince, thought I was going to docilely become his plaything, he was sadly mistaken! First wife or not, I refused to be part of a harem! I was his rank's equivalent, and I would have respect!

The men's faces were hard and blank. For a moment I thought they would rebel. Then Sven shouted: "Of course, Prince Alaric. To the Leader goes the best of the spoils. We all know that! Tell us something we don't know. The Princess Tara is as safe with us as if she were our sister. Now quit scowling up there and sit down so we can eat."

The rest of the men laughed and shouted agreement.

Alaric smiled at Sven's reply and led me to the table. "Sit, then, Tanista Tara of Eirlandia, and have your first Vike meal."

Chapter 2

I heard Alaric through the wood as I prepared for bed that evening. "Open the door, please. We need to talk."

Wrapping a robe around me, I opened the door halfway. "About what?" I asked.

I was tired and in no mood to talk. The supper had been tolerable, consisting mostly of fish with boiled tubers and some unfamiliar seasonings. It was well prepared, that I will admit. Obviously the ship's cook was skilled. But what I needed at the moment was to be away from all the men, the noise, and the smell. I needed to sleep and plan my escape back home.

I also wanted time alone to record the day's proceedings. Alaric had provided the room with a blank log book. I could only assume he knew I could read and write and that his informant had found out I kept a journal. I was grateful for the unknown person for imparting this knowledge, but I was also seething with anger that there was a traitor within my father's court.

Alaric looked both regal and frazzled. "We will be stopping tomorrow at a safe port, where we will stay for some days," he said. "I need to discuss my plans with you and to obtain your word on a few things. I know an Eirlandian's word is as good as a written contract, and I need such an agreement from you. It will save me much worry and your countrymen much grief and bloodshed. May I come in and sit down? The hall is no place to discuss such matters."

Backing away from the door, I gestured him in silently. I knew very well that this was all face-courtesy, and Alaric would do what he wished no matter what I said or did.

Best to get this over with so I could sleep. Giving my Honor Word to anything wasn't part of my plans, but I had no problem pretending to listen and say I would think on it.

He shut the door and walked straight to a small cupboard I had noticed but not touched. He brought out two glasses and a container of mead.

"Discussions are more civilized with drink to accompany them," he quoted from The Brehonia, a treatise on manners and hospitality all Eirlandians knew from childhood. Pouring two measures, he motioned me over to the more comfortable chair in the cabin.

"Tara, there is no easy way to say this," he began. "This raid was a different kind of mission. I came to capture you and other women around the same age as yours so they may become your maids in Vikland. You're in my custody as hostage, so the Vikes can be sure your people are going to behave themselves in the coming months."

I stared at him open-mouthed. "What are you talking about?"

"You are an act of indemnity against what we may have left in our wake with this raid." Alaric explained. "We do not seek war with your people. Indeed, we hope that our act in taking you may eventually lead to a lasting peace between our nations."

"I've got no more say over anyone's behavior than a dingle wildflower. People in Glin know me but I'm hardly a household name in other Eirlandian realms. You can be sure folks in the streets of Kilawey would frown if you asked them about me. What does my fate matter to the ArdRigh?"

The left eyebrow on his face hooked up. "You're known better than you might consider possible."

I could only offer an unbelieving smirk to his remark.

He went on. "My father has several men at the court of the ArdRigh. They have heard your name spoken around Kilawey many times the past few cycles. They heard talk that your father was soon going to be asked to bring you to Kilawey. You were to be formally presented to the High Court to be sworn as Tanista to the ArdRigh. That is, if you and the High Council had agreed."

The smirk vanished from my face. "You've got to be insane." I was shaking my head bewildered. "Either that or your father's men are terribly mistaken. Maybe they lie. Why would I be chosen as Tanista? My lineage is not that illustrious. I'm no relative to ArdRigh Brionston or his clan."

"What do you know of your mother?" he countered. "What do you know about the High Consort?"

I thought about his question for a minute before I answered. "My father and brother never spoke about my mother much. I do know she wasn't a native. She died in childbed when she bore me."

Alaric stayed silent, his face showing he waited for me to say more. "There were rumors she was Sidheran, but my father never acknowledged it to me. My brother claimed he was too young when she died to really remember her."

He sipped his mead, noting that I wasn't done yet.

"What has my mother got to do with this anyway? And what about the ArdRigh's consort? What does she have to do with anything? She takes little interest in the affairs of the country. I understand she was a political alliance with one of our allies, but that is about all I know."

I folded my arms and glared at him. He only chuckled.

"Relax and drink the mead, little eaglet. You'll get your answers. No need to ruffle your feathers at me. I had a feeling you didn't know your own family history, hence my question.

"Let me enlighten you then, something your father was remiss in not doing. I guess he didn't want to dwell in the past, and thought nothing would come of it. But something did come of it. In the light of your father's and brother's deaths, it's more crucial than it ever was."

The warmth of the mead made me relax. I could tell it was exceptional, being a product of the Hives of Muenstart.

If Alaric knew something important about my mother, I would be pleased to hear it. His words about my possibly becoming Tanista still made no sense. I was both intrigued by his revelations and confused. Why did my father not say anything to me about this? And why would I be considered a Tanista at all? I knew my brother and I were, in truth, half-siblings, and that my brother's mother had died in childbirth as mine had, but I had never really cared about that. We had been true siblings, I felt, and I knew I was loved just as any full sister would have been.

Alaric wiped his mouth. "Your mother was, indeed, Sidheran. In fact, she was a Principia of the Sidheran." The twinkle I'd seen in his eyes while trying to flee Glin was back. "She was also the sister of your current ArdRigh's consort, and niece of your ArdRigh Brionston's father."

I gave him the same disbelieving look as before but said nothing. That my mother was of the nobility was not surprising, as I could not see my father marrying beneath him. But a Principia? That would mean she was of the ruling class of the Sidheran. I had no reason to believe Alaric was lying, but part of me assumed his informants were mistaken. To my knowledge no high born Sidheran had mated with an Eirlandian in generations.

"It all gets a little complicated and I don't know all the ins and outs of the genealogy," he continued, "but apparently the Clan Boroumma has had connections with the Sidheran for several hundred years."

He poured himself more mead without offering me any. "This fact has been kept quiet by the Bards." He paused as if listening for someone or something. He went on, "So few beyond the immediate family know of this relationship. I guess it all happened during the Last Great War between the Sidheran and the Formorrid. According to the secret records my informants were able to obtain, your mother's clan was outnumbered and would have perished if the Clan Boroumma had not come to their rescue. The documents state that to honor their help, the Sidheran vowed that they would intermarry with the rulers of Eirlandia and that one day a member of a particular family of Sidheran and a member of the Clan Boroumma would produce a special prodigy, one destined to rescue both nations from certain extinction. You, Tara, from all anyone has been able to piece together, are that person."

I just about choked on the mead. "What? I'm no one special, I promise you. If I had been, why, my father would've told me. What kind of reason could he have to keep it a secret?"

My mind was awhirl yet again. How could this looked-for progeny be me? I wasn't special in any way I was ever told about. Yes, I had an ear for languages and I picked up mage work fairly easily, but I was hardly an extraordinary practitioner for my age! This whole thing didn't seem to make sense. But, obviously, the Vikes believed the story, to the point that they kidnapped me, apparently for political advantage.

"Protection," Alaric said as I processed these thoughts. He seemed to have an ear cocked at the door all the while he said it. "There are clan leaders who would have ordered you dead if they knew the truth of your family. You are heiress to a Sidheran heritage, and the rulers of both Eirlandia and Sidhera wanted you to grow up safe and in ignorance. That way your actions wouldn't betray your ancestry. Not even by accident."

After a sip, he dropped his voice and leaned forward in his chair. "Also, I don't believe even your father knew the extent of your parentage until recently, when he received the notice from the ArdRigh to bring you to Kilawey by Bellantine Eve."

Alaric's words scared me more than I let on. Although it was some time yet before the great Spring festival, I could not help but wonder why I had not yet been told of the upcoming journey. It did make me wonder, however, if the journey my father and brother had taken had had something to do with summons. Unfortunately, I realized, that was one question for which I would never have an answer.

Alaric put down his mead and crossed to me. "I have put myself at great risk in telling you all this," he said. "If others learn who and what you are, I'm not sure I can protect you. You are a great asset to your people and greater detriment to ours. If you had reached Kilawey and learned what you needed to become Tanista, the plans of several generations of Vikes would come to naught. Thus the raid on Glin; to secure you before your father could bring you to Kilawey. We had to stop you coming into your rightful inheritance."

"Prince Alaric," I said softly, my voice heavy with warning, "I appreciate your honesty. What you say makes little true sense to me, but that might be because this possibility was never discussed or even hinted." I stood up, forcing him back away from me. "If I am your captive, and as valuable as you claim, then you must realize that I cannot give you any assurances that I will not attempt to return to my people if given any opportunity."

Alaric's eyes opened wide. It was obvious he had not expected this reaction. "You have more self-control than other women I have met. I suppose that's because of your training as well as your heritage, whether you realize it or not. He reached out and slowly cupped my chin. "You are part Sidheran, Tara, and your otherworldliness captured my attention the moment I saw you.

Something in his eyes and voice warned me things were about to get out of hand if I allowed this conversation to go further.

I shook my head and put out my hand flat against his chest. "This is the mead talking," I declared. "Do not come any closer."

He reached out and grabbed at my hand, I struggled as he attempted to pull me closer. I could smell both mead and whiskey on his breath, and realized he had much more to drink after I had retired to my chambers.

"No," I cried out. "You will not do this! I claim Captive Right. I'm the same or superior rank than you; you cannot do this without consent."

Writhing furiously, I finally broke his hold and backhanded him as hard as I could. His head snapped to the side, loosening his grip.

Taking advantage of this short reprieve, I backed away, grabbing a stout pitcher that stood on a table behind me. Hefting the weapon, I continued. "If I am all you say I am, Alaric of Vikland, then you have no right to treat me as a common captive. Leave here, now. We can continue this discussion when you behave as your rank requires." I pulled myself as tall as I could and concentrated on appearing as regal as possible.

Alaric rubbed his cheek and jaw and shook his head. "I was warned about you." He looked at me sheepishly. "I guess I should've listened harder. My apologies, Lady, I let the moment get ahead of my manners."

He inched backwards and rose. "We will reach our harbor by early morning. We will be going ashore for some time while I await instructions from my father. You will be guarded and will have the run of the Dun as long as you don't try an escape or get messages through to your people. We're going someplace where my people hold sway, so you will have no allies to help you. The sooner you accept your status of honored captive, the happier you will be." He wobbled his jaw as he started for the door.

"Good night, Tara, I hope you sleep well. You will be served breakfast here in the cabin. I will come to get you when we are ready to depart the ship. Have your things packed neatly and dress appropriately to your station. I will have Vilk bring you the dress I wish you to wear tomorrow when he comes with your breakfast." With that he opened the door and went through. I heard the key in the lock turning. I was truly a captive for the night.

Sitting on the furs that were arranged on the bed, I took several deep, shuddering breaths. My mind tried to keep me calm and rational, as my Drui mage training had taught me. But too many things had happened too quickly to me, and my center was out of balance and my emotions held sway. Laying down and stifling my sobs in the pillows, I thought about my father and brother, my life as a whole in Eirlandia, my mother, even though I never knew her, and a thousand and one other things. I remembered warm summer nights spent in the garden at the main palace, the stars bright and twinkling, with the moon shining silver on the leaves of the elder trees, turning them a pale blue in the light.

I remembered my brother teaching me how to fight with dagger, bow and arrow, and staff. Our swords were all too large and heavy for me, but I became very adept at the other weapons, even besting my brother and his trainer at staves, much to their chagrin. I smiled a little at that memory. I recalled how proud my brother sounded when he recounted the incident to my father at evening meal that night.

I remembered, too, the look on my father's face when I announced I was going to enter into the kingdom-wide tourney for the best weapons handler. I would compete in staff, knife and shooting, I had declared. There was no rule against my entering, and I saw no reason not to compete against the best. Winning was not the goal, I told him, the goal was to see how good I really was.

"I can disguise myself," I remembered telling my father. "No one need know who I am, so they can compete as if against anyone. I want no special favors."

My father, I recalled, seemed dubious at first. But as the days wore on and he observed my skill first hand, he finally agreed to let me compete. I was outfitted as a huntress, as that was a normal occupation for outdoorsy women. I tied a scarf about my head to hide my hair, and wore a covering over my nose and mouth. This, too, was common in such contests so that the judges would not know the identity of the contestants, which helped to ensure impartiality.

The contest was long and arduous, to be sure. It took some time to whittle down the field until there were only three of us left. The target was set up at the farthest reach of our arrows. No quarter was given for sex, size or age. My two opponents were both male, taller and stronger than I was. I do not think my father thought I would win, or at least not come in first.

But the other two were not a skilled with bow as I, and their shots, while very good, were not dead center. Sighting for the small space between the two other arrows in the exact center of the target, I had sent a fleeting prayer to, of all people, my mother, to steady my hand and strengthen my arm. Then I loosed the arrow and watched as it hit exactly center of the target, sending everyone, including my father, to their feet in amazement. I remember looking back and seeing my father smiling more widely than I had ever witnessed before. He gestured to the target and nodded in acknowledgement of my victory. I had never felt prouder than at that moment.

These thoughts passed through me, and soon the tears were shed and exhaustion took its toll. I cannot honestly remember when I fell asleep. But I know that it did not seem long enough.

Vilk knocked as soon as sunrise came and slightly opened the door.

"My lady, good morning. I brought you some breakfast and a change of clothing. May I enter?"

"Come in, Vilk," I answered, climbing out of bed and putting on my morning robe. "Morning greetings." That his voice was so low pitched still surprised me, but it was very melodious, and hinted that there was a foreign land and language in his past.

I pointed at the table from which I had grabbed the pitcher the night before. "I cleared up that space. You may set the food down there."

Vilk walked in with the tray and a gown draped over his arms. He put down the tray and held out the gown. "Alaric says you are to wear this, Lady. You are to have breakfast, get dressed, and make sure you are packed. I will help as you need. I have some experience with women's clothing."

He noticed my raised eyebrow. His cheeks turned faintly red, but he met my eyes easily enough. "I was a merchant before I was captured many years ago. I'd help women customers try on clothes sometimes."

I kept my expression schooled. The fact he had been a captive explained many things. This man was not, I was now certain, born a Vike. He, like myself, had been born somewhere very different. I did not want to surprise or embarrass him with any comment.

"When the Vikes took me, they found my warrior skills better than they expected," he continued. "They also found I was a bit different. I became chief guard for female prisoners, once the Vikes came to understand that I had no interest in women in bed."

"Oh, I see," I spoke with a neutral tone. "You are Ardinard, then?"

"Yes, I am from Greecia, where this is commonplace. Not so much amongst the Eirlandian and Vike I know, but not unknown. Eirlandia at least accepts how I am without fuss. I never stay long in Vikland, as they don't accept so easily."

I sat down and lifted the lid of the dish to see what he'd brought me. It smelled delicious and looked appetizing. "Well, I for one am glad to have someone onboard that I need not worry about wanting more of me than I wish to give." Vilk smiled slightly in response and nodded before turning away. With no more ado, I broke my fast.

Vilk put the gown down on the bed and tidied up the room while I ate. When I had finished, I rose and washed as well as I could. There was, of course, a pitcher and ewer in the cabin, along with a bar of soap and a towel. It was hardly the standard I was used to, but I made do.

Surprisingly, the room boasted a full-length mirror. I stood for a moment in my night dress, trying to picture myself as a man would see me. I knew I was slightly taller than average for an Eirlandian female. My hair coloring was, I had been told, the color of burnished bronze and was, at the moment, freely flowing down to just past my waist.

Normally it was tied back and braided, or even done up very fancifully if I was in court. But now it was free of constraints, and in serious need of a good brushing and taming. My green eyes stared back at me, and I saw the slighted curve of my eyelids, which hinted at my apparent Sidheran ancestry. I looked a bit older than my sixteen summers, and most took me for a couple of years older, but that had often been more a help than hindrance as all the eligible males assumed I was already betrothed so their flirting was never serious. My father had always told me I would never be forced into marriage for political reasons. 'Well, I guess that's about to change,' I thought to myself. Turning away from the mirror, I crossed to where the gown lay waiting.

The gown was a light green, with scalloping that looked like waves on the neckline, sleeves, and hem. A soft material I could not place, laced the sides without interrupting the patterning on the front and back. An undercoat was already attached to the outer dress, so I had only to slip it on and all was done. With Vilk turned away of his own accord, I slipped out of my sleeping dress and put the gown on.

At my request, Vilk turned and did up the side lacings, which I could never have managed myself. He also brushed out my hair and pinned it up in a way I had not seen before, and assumed it was a Vike style. It suited me and the gown, however, so I let it be. I had never been one to believe that because someone is an enemy that their culture has nothing good about it.

Curious, I asked him about the clothing.

"Is this the clothing style in Vikland, Vilk?" I asked in a light tone. "And do Vike women really do up their hair in such an elaborate fashion all the time? Or only special occasions?"

Vilk smiled slightly, his brown eyes twinkling. "The dress is only worn by high nobility," he answered. "The hairstyle was a favorite of Prince Alaric's mother, although I must say it becomes you just as well."

Finally, he brought forth some slippers that matched the dress, but were sturdy enough for walking or riding. I smiled and put them on, letting him lace them around my ankle, another style I had not seen. But they were comfortable and handsome and hardly even seen under the gown.

We had just finished, when a knock came at the door. "Tara, are you ready?" It was Sven. "Alaric needs to know how much longer you need."

"I must finish packing," I called back. "I've only just finished breakfast and put on the gown."

At that I heard Sven chuckle. "Vilk," he called through the door, "how does she look?"

Vilk glanced at me and smiled somewhat impishly. "As good as a statue of Freya," he called back.

Blushing just a bit at the compliment, although I wasn't certain who Freya was, the implication was clear, I stopped Vilk from saying anything further with a sharp look.

"Tell Alaric he's rushing things a bit and if he wanted me ready by now, he should've sent breakfast earlier. However, I should be done packing within a candle mark.

Sven chuckled somewhat loudly. "Very good. I will see you topside shortly." I heard him retreat down the corridor and smiled. I could hear from his voice that Sven was genuinely surprised and pleased.

"Best be to packing, Lady," Vilk said. "Must be ready on time or Prince Alaric gets upset."

"Posh on Prince Alaric" I retorted. "I will be on time because I said I would be. I'm not afraid of Alaric's temper. He has more reason to be afraid of mine." I smiled slightly to take the sting away.

His puzzled expression told me Alaric had not mentioned his retreat from my chambers the night before to anyone. "Don't worry, it doesn't matter. Let's finish packing, it's all but done anyway."

In less than a candle mark I sent Vilk to let Sven know. As I awaited his return, I took out my mother's necklace. In the early morning light it gleamed pale. Its light blue surface shimmered and I glimpsed, for the first time, a tiny pattern emanating from the center of the stone.

'There, my love,' I remembered Nurse telling me all the years ago when she placed it round my neck. 'There, keep this stone. It was the only thing of Sidhera your mother had. 'Tis a shame she wore it not when you were born, or she would still be alive. Lifenstone, they call this gem, bringer of life and light. Wear this always, and show it to no one, including your father. It is given mother to daughter down a line and has always been so since first the Sidheran walked the shores of this land. It comes from a place and time far, far away where, they say, magical things abounded and the Sidheran knew how to command the elements themselves.'

She had made sure the chain was long enough not to be seen under my clothes.

Footsteps came down the hall outside and I quickly tucked away the stone. The voices of my past faded into the voices of my present.

There was a perfunctory knock, before Alaric entered, carrying a large cloak and hood.

"Put this on," he ordered. The weather is not at its best, and I don't want the gown wetted and ruined before we come to the Dun. Make sure the hood is completely up, it will cover your face, but just look down. I will guide you to the carriage and out again. It is good you are ready early. The journey will take a little longer than I hoped."

As he was speaking, Vilk silently helped me with the cloak, and made sure the hood was pulled up properly and smoothly. The young Vilk's eyes reflected the worried tone in Alaric's voice, and I knew that there was more to this stop than Alaric had let on. Exactly how much more I was to learn, much to my surprise and chagrin.

Chapter 3

Each moment riding to the Dun was a battle. The carriage rocked furiously, as if sailing a hurricane, threatening to depose me from my seat. I clung as the chilly wind beat at me. The rain stung my face, even through the hood, like little needles of ice.

As soon as we entered the courtyard of the Dun, the wind's icy anger mellowed, and something told me there was more at work here than high stone walls to shield this place against the harsh weather.

Bracing myself against a wet splash of rainwater as I dismounted, I was surprised to land on dry ground. Glancing up, I saw the telltale shimmer of magic arching above the courtyard. The place was warded against harsh weather with a strong weather magic spell. Looking quickly side to side, I noticed that even the walls glimmered, some magic resided there as well, but I had no idea what type of magic one would use on outdoor walls, unless it was to strengthen the stone again weathering. I tried to take in more of my surroundings, but Alaric lead me on with urgency and it was all I could do to keep the great cloak on me from tripping my feet.

There was a hurried echo of our footsteps before Alaric slid off my hood and I stared bewildered at uniformly dark walls. Nothing about this stronghold matched Eirlandian or Vike styles. The ceiling was too high to be visible. The only thing I could see were feathery ringlets of light drooping from globes whose chains were invisible too, no matter how hard I tried to make them out.

When I looked before me, my throat almost choked with fear. About fifty steps away a dais made of the same stone as the walls held a wooden throne displaying a marking in dark red.

The thing which sat on the throne leaned its neck out from between its shoulders as it regarded me through eyes surrounded by lurid scales. It was the strangest creature I'd ever seen. It was tall, that was obvious even though it was seated. I learned later it was male, but truly could not tell because of the clothing and the fact it had very reptilian features.

The clothing itself was almost ludicrous by Eirlandian standards. A starched white ruff surrounded its neck. The shoulders of the robes were stiff with gems and gold and extended out past where I assumed the actual shoulders were. The sleeves of the garment were full and tightly cuffed at the wrist, where almost claw-like hands extended. Six-fingered, the hands were scaled and each digit bore at least one ring and long lethal-looking nails. Since it was sitting, I could only assume it was normally proportioned and it obviously had two legs and feet, since jeweled slippers peaked out from the bottom of the several layers of robes.

Its face looked scaly, almost fish-like. It had a normal looking mouth, and when it spoke, it did so with no real difficulty. Its words were understandable, but with an accent I could not place.

"Prince Alaric of Vike," the scaly creature spoke, "we welcome you and your men. The identity of your guest had not been revealed. I cannot say we are pleased, but we will abide by our arrangement." The thing paused, eyeing me solemnly. "Should my people learn of her sojourn here, it could become unpleasant for her. See that your men guard her at all times."

This deliberate snub of my presence confused me. I opened my mouth to protest, but Alaric grabbed my arm and shoved me backwards toward Vilk and Sven.

"It will be as you say, Emissary Borrmid. The girl is our political prisoner and is here only because we could not keep her in Eirlandia and did not have the provisions for an uninterrupted voyage to Vikland. We await word from my father, and the supplies for our ship, then we will be off. The girl will be kept away from you and your people. She is harmless in any case. She has neither training nor even knowledge of her ancestry. She is no threat to you and yours."

"Be it as you say, Prince" the emissary responded. "Take yourselves now to the guest quarters at the far northern end. You know the way from times before. Your men are there and you may have complete use of that section of the Dun. It includes a private entrance and exit, as you know, and even a garden, although it is still too early in the season for much to be growing."

Having said so, he stood and made his way down from the dais and through a door set into the wall to our right that I had not even noticed before.

When Alaric looked at me it was with warning in his eyes. Something was going on here, I realized. The tension beneath the surface exchange was obvious. Then he led the way back as we had come, turning left when we came to the entryway.

As soon as we turned, he spoke a single word I could not even begin to pronounce, and the great hall went dark behind us. My eyes went wide. I didn't know anyone possessed such magical devices. The ability to create such things was thought lost in the many wars between the Formorrid and the Sidheran. So, my teachers had been drastically wrong about that part of my history lessons.

"That opprobrious creature should shield himself from common sight lest it become unpleasant for him," I sniffled.

"Keep your voice down," Alaric said. "Do not assume these walls are soundproof. The walls around us were the same black substance as in the chamber. I wondered if it really was stone.

"In case you wondered, I'm very curious as to why I'm not welcome. That ugly thing in there didn't blush a mite with his uncivility. Actually, I doubt you'd ever catch him blush anyway for his nauseating complexion."

"They all look like that." "They must. Who was he?" "A Formorrid chieftain."

I ground to a halt. "What did you say?"

"Don't stop here." Alaric pulled me into motion again, leading me through the convoluted route to our part of the Dun.

"The Formorrid are no more." My voice was strained with disbelief. "Who said?"

"My teachers."

"They're terribly mistaken, now hush up and follow me."

Alaric said nothing as I wondered about the identity of our host. We reached the Vike part of the Dun within about a candle mark, I judged, and the walls suddenly went from the black material to normal stone and wood. The central chamber we entered looked like it could have been anywhere in Eirlandia, except for the Vikland tapestries along the walls.

Still silent, Alaric motioned for us to proceed across the hall to a smaller door just past the main fire pit. This door led down a corridor with several rooms on either side. Alaric went through another door at the end of the corridor into a smaller version of the greater chamber we had left and indicated toward a door flanked by two Vike guards.

"Your suite of rooms" he told me. "Mine are across the way." Another guard stood outside the other door. "Vilk's been here before and he'll show you around. Settle in for now and I'll come within a large mark to accompany you to the central hall. You need to meet other members of the entourage."

My suite was quite grand, with fruit and drink waiting for me. The chamber led out into the garden, just like the reptilian emissary had said.

True to his word, Alaric came before the next major mark. This time warriors, courtiers, women of court and servants milled about the great hall. A few Eirlandian-looking girls were grouped together in a corner, while a Vike guard watched over them. 'They must be the other girls who'd been kidnapped,' I thought to myself. So I smiled at them, hoping to pass on a little encouragement. If they had really been rounded up in Eirlandia then they would be my personal maids soon.

Nodding to various faces, Alaric led me in silence to chairs at one end of the hall. Vilk assumed a vigilant stance by my side as I sat down and Alaric took a chair beside me, Sven standing close to him.

A gong rang out and a herald announced: "Prince Alaric now sits in council. Let all approach to hear and discuss." Courtiers, both male and female, and warriors approached where we sat.

One older gentleman stepped forward, looking like the chamberlain of the place. His features reminded me of the Formorrid, but they were softer, causing me to wonder if he was a hybrid of Formorrid and Vike.

He inclined his head toward us both then straightened. "My Lord Alaric, welcome back to DasDunFormorra. We are honored by your presence and assure you that you and your people will all be looked after in the tradition of our people."

After that he stepped aside to a place next to Alaric. Alaric stood and acknowledged the man. "My thanks and that of my men, Leifson. I have always enjoyed my stays here. This time I bring a special guest."

He gestured to me and I stood to express my courtesy. "May I present the erstwhile Tanista Tara of Kilbrae. The Tanista is now on her way to Vikland to meet my father and the court. Soon after she will become my betrothed."

The announcement sent round a low, threatening murmur. Alaric held up his hand. Silence returned.

"My father plans for her and me to be hand-fasted before Freyatine. Thus, we will have claim on the very throne of Kilawey!"

Shock rooted me to the spot. Hand-fasted? Against my will? Claim to Kilawey? The Vikes were mad! No Eirlandian council would confirm me as Tanista with a Vike mate! What was his father thinking to even propose such a thing? Could they be that ignorant of our laws? Or were they too pigheaded to think we would ever give in to such a travesty without rebelling? I glared at Alaric, but he did not look at me as he continued his announcement.

"Tanista Tara is guest-sacred and will be allowed the freedom of our part of the Dun. However, under orders of the Emissary of the Formorrid, she is not to set foot in any other part of the complex. She must not be harmed but turned away from any of the exits to the Dun unless I, Vilk or Sven accompany her."

Gesturing to the captured women, he continued. "These women are to be Tanista Tara's personal body servants and are also not to be harmed in any way. The penalties for doing so will be swift and severe.

"If we are to convince Kilawey of our honorable intentions, we must treat their people with respect. I will tolerate no disobedience in this matter," he concluded.

Then he turned to the girls and beckoned them forward. "You have come from Glin and if anyone here tries to harm you or even make a fool of you in any way, you are to tell Sven, my steward, immediately. I assure you that no harm will come to you because of it." Sven bowed to the assembled women.

"And now, ladies," Alaric went on, "please bring your mistress to her suites. Vilk, her steward, will show you your quarters. Have her prepared for formal supper one candle mark after sundown."

He turned to me and bowed with a sardonic smile. "My lady, I leave you to your women to rest and enjoy the rest of your day. I look forward to your company at supper."

Oh, I knew how this courtly game was played. I could say nothing in this place and at this time, but he would hear my thoughts on this little game.

"As you wish, my Lord Alaric." The snide barb was well disguised. "I look forward to our future discussions regarding this." Forcing the upper decibels out of my voice, I added softly, for his ears only, "Mind you these words as I leave: Beware setting a trap for the unknown prey, for they may end up being more than you bargained for."

Trying to look as regal as I could, I swept from the hall with Vilk before me and my ladies behind me. At the door I glanced back and was rewarded by the sight of a confused Alaric watching me.

Reaching my chambers, I dismissed my maids and Vilk, pleading a headache, which was really not so much a lie as an exaggeration. I could not undress, I knew, but I lay on the bed, with only my slippers off, to mull over the day so far.

It was obvious that the Formorrid and the Vikes are allies. It was also obvious that the Formorrid had use of great mage abilities, along with advanced techniques for creating objects, much more than our most advanced Drui scientists. It seemed the Formorrid were very wary of me and, I assumed, what I represented. Perhaps they feared that an alliance between Eirlandia and Vikland would put them in a vulnerable position.

'Well, little change of THAT happening,' I thought to myself. 'I will not allow myself to be a helpless tool in all this. Somehow I will escape, or at least get word back to Eirlandia that I am alive and being held captive.' My inner thoughts gave me strength and courage. I could almost hear my father's voice in the back of mind, telling me to be strong and to always find the advantage in any situation.

"Think like your opponent," I remembered him saying when he had beaten me at Hounds and Foxes. "Look at more than your pieces, look at the whole board and see what else is there you might have missed. These lessons are good for real life, not just games. Seek out your opponent's weaknesses and exploit them." His words echoing, I sat up and put on my slippers once again, checking myself in the mirror and patting down a stray hair or two. "He calls me 'BanRigh' and 'Tanista', I need to start acting like high royalty." I muttered. When the knock came at the door, I opened it, and smiled at Vilk who stood waiting. Without another word, I gestured him to lead the way, as I silently took in my surroundings, determined to learn as much of this place as I could.

Supper that night was interminable, but exceptional. The tables were a panoply of Vike and Eirlandian dishes whereas the mead tasted immensely superior to any I could recall. But I gazed at the reveling faces as if from behind a mask. Almost swamped by a dress much fancier and heavier than what I'd had on before, I longed for my trews and overskirt. That used to be my freedom at home.

Then again, this was pretty much a state dinner, like the ones that happened at home. Everyone came to gawk at the Eirlandian Tanista BanRigh. Even though I had not been confirmed in that title, and probably never would be, these people seemed to think the title was mine. Both male and female courtiers attempted to draw me into conversation. My responses did not range past nods while beside me Alaric spoke of military matters with a man who looked like a commander of a Vike fleet.

He spoke Vike, oblivious that I was reasonably fluent in the language. His spies had no reason to suspect me, since I'd taken pains to hide my knowledge from everyone but my tutor, whom I had begged to teach me. Understanding the language of the raiders meant a better bargain on the day we might sign a peace with each other.

High Eirl had been the first language of our people, but no one spoke it around the Eirlandian kingdoms except scholars laboring on old texts of our ancestors. I understood it too. Knowledge of the first language also revealed the thinking of the Drui. They were rumored to practice the Sidheran arts in secret far from the towns, inside caves and stone towers. I had yet to learn how my knowledge of archaic speech and writing would serve me.

Dinner ended and Alaric rose, lifting me up gently by my elbow with him.

"Good people, we bid you good night. The *hosagge* (a word I knew meant hostage) is no doubt tired. I will accompany her to her quarters and stay awhile. Please, continue your refreshment and entertainment. I will see you for council tomorrow one mark after first meal." He escorted me to the suites and dismissed my maids.

Motioning me into a chair, he poured himself some more mead and settled on a stool. "I am sure you have many questions, Little Eagle," he said. "Ask away. I wish you to fully understand what is happening before we leave for Vikland some weeks hence."

I trembled with suppressed rage. "How dare you?" I fought the urge to shout. "How dare you show me off like some prize antlers and have the audacity to proclaim we will hand-fast before Freyatine, whenever that might be. Do you think I am going to agree to this travesty? Do you believe Kilawey would ever confirm me as Tanista after they find out I contracted with a Vike? Are you and your father delusional? Insane? Or does your pride rend you from reality?"

Raising the mead to his mouth, Alaric paused. He set the drink down, and stared at me.

"I am my own person," I continued. "I decide who has thigh-right, no one else. Not you, not your father, not even my ArdRigh. I will not marry you. I will marry for love, and for no other reason. My father knew this and respected it. If I am to be Tanista, I will consort with someone I respect. Someone who understands the privileges and duties of a consort. You, Vike, are not that man."

In my rage I did not see Alaric's eyes beginning to harden, nor his bemusement turning to anger.

"I may be your pampered prisoner, Prince Alaric, but I will never, ever be your partner. I owe that much to my people. I will not betray them and grant you a foothold in Eirlandia, no matter how precarious."

"Enough," Alaric roared. "I have had enough of your temper, woman. You are my prisoner, as you so admit. As such you are under my laws. I do not need your consent to hand-fast with you. You are already mine under Vike law. You are breewif, a wife by conquest. I intend make you my Truwif, my true wife, by the hand-fast ceremony. If you do not wish that, so be it. But your rights as an Eirlandian don't stand while you are here or when you go to Vikland."

He crossed over to me and stood over me in a posture of dominance.

"The women in Vikland do not have 'thigh-right' as you call it. They do as their husband commands. They give their favors to only him. Your status will be greater if we take terms to your ArdRigh as a couple hand-fasted. It would put you in a position to help your people."

Alaric swept his blond hair from his eyes. He continued: "We would contract, at least at first, for only the Anu, the one year. That will be enough time for my father's plan to come to fruition anyway. Once our plans are done, whether you are my Truwif or not will make no difference."

His voice went softer, suddenly, and I could see he was regretting his outburst. He backed up, but did not sit again. "You are distraught, and I was cruel just then, I apologize. I want us to be happy, Tara, whether you believe that at this moment or not. I hope you understand that I am only doing as my father and my king command me. We are strangers, I get that. I'm not in the habit of forcing myself on women, captives or no. But you need to understand that, willing or not, this is what is in store for you. Our lives are not important, our happiness with each other is not important. What is important is peace between our peoples."

He walked out before I could gather my wits enough to reply. I stood shaking in that room. Soon tears spurted from my eyes in silence. I cried for my father and brother, for my land, and for me.

Taking out my mother's pendant, I whispered to it softly, in High Eirl. "Oh, mother, I wish I had the legendary power of your people. I wish I knew what's best for everyone right now. Why do I have to figure it out as it happens? I might make a wrong choice...I dread it..."

The stone seemed to glow for a moment then it dulled. A sudden calm settled in my bosom. "Mother?" I whispered again in the old tongue. "Are you somehow here?"

The glow of the stone reappeared, brighter this time. The next instant a sudden beam of light shot forth from it and coalesced into a vague female shape about two feet away from me.

"Daughter," I heard a female voice in the shape, "at last you have learned how to call forth the wisdom of the Lifenstone. It has been a long time since last I saw you. I have watched you grow and I am proud of who you have become and who you will become. There is much to teach you before you reach Vikland shores. Hear me now well and remember. You have much to learn and scant time to learn it."

I sank to my knees, slowly crossing my legs on the floor. My sight of the present dimmed and paths I'd never seen opened up before me. Unforeseen yet not unfamiliar, they welcomed me. My mother was there. I knew it without being told.

"Tara, my darling girl," my mother's voice appeared around me. Suddenly the shape from before appeared. The image was vague, as if I saw through a gossamer curtain, but I knew it was her.

"I waited until I knew the prophecy was beginning," she told me. "Come, sit here," suddenly there was a comfortable bench with cushions. Almost in a daze, I sat down with her beside me, even though the veil was still there.

"I know you have many questions, Eaglet," she said, echoing the words of Sven and Alaric when I was captured, I realized. "I can show you in pictures better than words the answers," she went on. "But you must not write of this, for this knowledge is sacred and not to be known by just anyone. I must take you on a journey to the past, but I must also teach you skills that come from your ancestors. These things must be kept close to your heart. You will know when to use them. Then she touched my forehead and I found myself transported into the past. As instructed I write no more about this, except to say that these skills and knowledge would prove crucial in the future.

Four large candle marks later, I awoke from this strange state. Surprisingly refreshed and calm, I went to the inner door of the suite. Spying Vilk on duty, I gestured to him to come in.

"I was deep in thought and lost track of time." I told him. That was the truth. "Please help me off with this dress. I wish to sleep." Vilk quickly helped me out of the cumbersome gown.

He turned down the bed and indicated the dressing gown and robe. "May your dreams bring you peace," he said softly. He looked at me in a strange way before walking out of the room.

I slipped into the dressing gown and climbed into bed. My rest that night was deep, but I feel even more knowledge was imparted to me, although I could never remember anything specific.

Chapter 4

I will be the first to admit that it was not always easy to fully embrace the fate my mother had shown me in my vision. I was still in mourning for the things that had been, and part of me still rebelled at the idea of being forced to marry someone purely for political reasons.

I decided I would give him opportunity to show me what kind of man he truly was. It appeared my fate was foretold, but there was no indication as to how long it would take to fulfill that fate. I didn't intend to betray my true self, but if I could also become his true life-mate at some time in the future, so much would be to the better.

Thus it was that Alaric was very confused by my behavior the next several days. He found me unfailingly kind and courteous. At one point, as we stood in the small garden the Vike quarters had, Alaric coughed softly and stepped slightly closer. "Tara, I hope you are comfortable enough here. I am sorry I have not seen much of you lately. I have been very busy sorting out diplomatic things between our people here and the Formorrid, as well as sending and receiving messages from home.

"It is fine," I told him. "The ladies you gave me are very talkative and we spend much time speaking about our old lives in Eirlandia, and speculating what awaits us in Vikland."

"Such as?" Alaric inquired. "Oh, things like what we would be doing this time of year if we were home. I was pleased to learn that some of ladies were from educated families, so with them I discuss politics and history, as well as poetry and art."

Alaric's reaction to this was almost comical. "I see…" he said, obviously seeing nothing. "What strange lives the women of Eirlandia lead. In our land, very few women learn more than rudimentary writing and reading. They are schooled in the practical arts of managing households, animal husbandry, farming, sewing and weaving. We have little time for gentle pursuits. Our lives are harsher than Eirlandians, just as our land and weather is harsher."

"Oh," I answered. "I know little about Vikland and its people. You must tell me more before we reach your homeland."

Thus it was we spent many an hour discussing the cultural differences between our two countries. I believe these times helped me become more understanding of the Vikes and their culture. While their spiritual beliefs were similar to ours, their gods and goddesses had very different personalities, most were almost hostile to mortals, whereas ours were kind and wise and did all they could to make us mortals have the best lives we could.

Alaric told me much of life among the Vikes, their laws, their religious beliefs, and their attitudes toward women. It was only the last that I had a problem understanding. Women among the Vikes were not treated equally, and did not have the same rights under law unless they happened to be a widow with no sons. Women could be warriors only if they stood beside their husbands to defend their land, or opted to go raiding, but since women were usually not wanted on board Vike ships, that usually only happened if either the commander had a Truwif who wished to go raiding, or he managed to find a crew that had several wives who wished to participate. Not a frequent occurrence.

I told him about my childhood, and about the life and laws of the Eirlandia he did not know. Although he had heard reports from this father's spies, through me he glimpsed everyday life.

We spent much time in lively but respectful debate about Eirlandian laws regarding the rights of females. Alaric actually came to admit that our laws made better sense in many ways.

One such time was at a luncheon that we two had privately. Vilk stood watch outside the small eating chamber, but the two of us were alone. I admit I was a bit nervous about this at first, but Alaric played the part of a perfect courtier.

He served me delicacies I had read about but never tasted before, explaining in detail how they were prepared and the history of the dishes. One such was small slivers of a fish he called trout, which was served cold and obviously raw, but whose taste was incredible.

"This fish is only served at special meals," I remember him telling me.

"It seemed to me that lately we have begun to truly know each other, and each other's culture. I am grateful for all you have taught me, Tara. I hope you have learned somethings of us that are not too disagreeable.

I smiled at his words, and decided I liked this side of my would-be husband. "I have come to the realization that this part of my life is something that the Awen has planned for me," I confided. "I need to understand you and your people, Alaric. If I'm to live among them, then I need to understand the culture, how they think, what they believe, how they behave."

Alaric's face had turned questioning as soon as I mentioned the Awen. "What or who is this 'Awen'?" he asked. "I have not heard the term."

"The Awen is what you might call 'Fate'," I replied. "It the great Pattern that governs the universe and all who exist within it. We have choice, mind you, but the Awen is aware of the outcome of each decision made and does what it can to guide us on the best path for our lives."

"Aah, the Weavers," he replied knowingly. "Yes, we have much the same thing in our culture. Please, go on."

"I know my first few days on the ship and even the first few days here were rough. You must remember that I was taken by force from all that I had ever known. My family was murdered, and even though you had no part in that, it was still your people who did the deed. I was in shock, in mourning, somewhat terrified and unwilling to show it. Now I am beginning to understand what is happening and beginning to believe that what you propose might actually come true."

Alaric didn't answer me in words. He simply reached across the table and took hold of my hands. I could feel his strength and support, and a wave of some emotion I couldn't identify washed over me. I suddenly felt completely safe and knew I wanted to keep that feeling no matter what happened.

One day, a few days after the luncheon, while we sat in the small garden, surrounded by trees that showed the first shafts of flowers, Alaric took my face in his hands. "Tara, I know not what has changed you, but I love the change." He bent forward and kissed me gently on the lips.

I'll admit to surprise, but there was not a feeling of animal passion surrounding him. The kiss, while on the lips, was almost chaste. It was tentative, as if he was slowly feeling his way down an unknown path.

In a way, I suppose he was. While I will admit to feeling somewhat more at ease with him, and there were times that his company was welcomed and very interesting, I was still a long way from wanting anything further than companionship.

On that occasion, I was saved from anything more than a kiss by the arrival of Sven at the entrance to the garden. I could tell from his expression that he was both pleased and annoyed at the scene.

Clearing his throat loudly, he proceeded to walk towards us. Alaric pulled away quickly and turned toward his old friend, a questioning look on his face.

"Alaric, excuse me for intruding, but there are some matters that have come to my attention that warrant your presence. It seems the Formorrid are becoming more and more upset with the presence of our guest, and are demanding we leave as soon as possible. I can't seem to get them to listen to me, so I thought you might have better luck.

I'm happy to keep Tara company while you deal with our hosts. For all I'm your second in command, they seem to regard me as some sort of lackey who has no authority whatsoever."

Sven looked at me sideways as he said this, and the quirk to his mouth spoke volumes regarding how he felt about the situation.

Alaric sighed heavily, almost comically. "Alright, then, let me go see what this is all about. I will take you up on your offer, Sven, to keep Lady Tara company while I'm gone. Perhaps you and she can get to know each other better. After all, you and she will be in close contact once we reach Vikland. I'm sure you know more about the day-to-day workings of the High Court than I do.

Sven smiled slyly at me, then put on a more somber face for his friend. "Of course, my Prince," he said, in a somewhat teasing tone. "Tara and I can exchange knowledge about our two countries and cultures. Perhaps we can even exchange notes regarding the behavior of certain members of the royal family."

Alaric did not respond to this quip, and I could tell it was a conversation that had occurred many times between the two friends. Instead Alaric simply bowed to me, raised a fist to his friend, and strode out of the garden.

Turning to me, Sven gestured to the chamber door. "This old sea dog has a problem in flora," he said lightly. "Would my lady object to going back inside and sitting near a fireplace? There's a chamber I know of that is not often used, but is open to people seeing who is inside. We can talk in private and will not be heard, but people will be able to see us clearly as they pass in the hallway, so no one can gossip about what might be going on behind our backs."

I remember laughing at that quip. It sounded much like what my father used to say to female guests when he wanted a private word about something that wasn't for everyone's ears.

"I think some time before a fire conversing with you is a wonderful idea," I answered.

The older Vike smiled and led down a hallway I had been through before. Within a few minutes we were ensconced beside a warm fire, mead in hand. A few pieces of bread and fruit were also within reach, and the feeling of the room was inviting yet also private.

Leaning back into the chair, Sven eyed me over the rim of his goblet.

"So, Tara, tell me truthfully, are you and Alaric becoming better acquainted and are you more at ease with what is going on and what will be happening in the near future?"

"I am, in truth, more comfortable with Alaric." I replied. "He has more layers to him than I imagined at first. I think he feels the weight of the responsibility placed upon him by his father strongly. He is a raider, so having to behave as a courtier is difficult for him at times."

"That is true," Sven acknowledged. "Alaric has spent most of his life outside of court, tending to his father's fleet and learning the ways of the sea. The king and his court is too tame for Alaric's personality. He is very hands-on, and diplomacy is something he is not yet well skilled or versed in."

I smiled. I had noticed that about the man and told Sven so.

"I can imagine," Sven agreed. "Alaric is actually not as lusty as many of his men, or even his peers. His late mother took pains to impress upon him the idea that women have ideas and knowledge and skills of their own that are just as valuable and just as important as any man. Before her death, she made sure Alaric understood that not all women were his for the taking just because of his status."

I stayed silent. Alaric had never once mentioned his mother to me. He also never talked much about his father, nor mentioned any other siblings, so I assumed that such things were not spoken of to outsiders.

"Alaric must never know I told you about his mother," cautioned Sven. "It is not something that is normally discussed or spoken about. It is our belief that speaking of the dead can bring bad consequences. I sometimes think it nonsense, but such is the Vike way. It is also the same reason he will not speak about siblings. He had an older brother and younger sister at one time, but both died from a terrible illness, the same one that took the queen."

"I am sorry for his loss and that of his family and your whole tribe," I answered.

"As I am for the loss of your father and brother," said Sven softly. "I know you understand that Alaric had nothing to do with that raid. Indeed it was undertaken by some outlaws without any official sanction or knowledge. I understand the culprits have been found and punished for their crime."

"Punished how?" I asked, almost dreading the answer. Tales of the cruelty of Vike punishments were told often around the fires in the Dark Time.

"They were banished," Sven said matter-of-factly. "Their ships were taken, their bounty seized, and the captain and first mate were set adrift in a small boat with food and water for five days. If they are ever found in Vike waters or territory again they will be killed."

The punishment was much in line with our laws, I realized. Eirlandians never outright killed their own, even criminals. But those who had severely flouted the law were banished and outlawed. It seemed the Vike had similar ideas.

The conversation then took a brighter turn as Sven began to regale me with tales of Alaric's boyhood adventures. In return I told him of my life in my father's court, and a few of the girlhood mishaps and victories I experienced, including my tale of The Unknown Huntress, which sprang from my participation in that long-ago contest I had remembered weeks before on the ship.

Before either of us realized, hours had passed and Vilk finally found us to say dinner was waiting and Alaric was almost beside himself with worry as no one seemed to know where we were.

Needless to say, Alaric and Sven had words just out of hearing range after dinner. I don't know what was said, but Sven gave me a small smile and wink before he left, and Alaric was a bit more subdued than earlier.

Pleading weariness, I went to my chambers shortly after dinner ended and quickly sunk into sleep.

Chapter 5

I slewed across the border of sleep into wakefulness. The hour was well past midnight and I was never in the habit of waking up in the middle of the night. Unless…yes, the reason became clear a moment later. I wasn't alone in my chamber.

Something moved in the darkness. I lay still and listened. The urge to throw off the sheets and shout that there was an intruder in my room took me by force, but I kept up my hoarse breathing pretending to snore.

My racing heart slowed as I concentrated in the darkness. A very subdued yet deep gurgling rose from a far corner of the room. Someone was standing near the bundles of my belongings. As I angled myself, ever so gently, to make out the shape lurking in that corner of my room, I heard a sudden low burst of impatience. It was quickly repressed.

The intruder moved away from the bundles and over to another corner of the room and that's when I saw its tall shape in the dimness. Something about the way it moved its head brought back a shocking realization. It couldn't have been anyone but the fish-like creature, the Formorrid emissary with whom Alaric had convened soon after our arrival in this land.

Why had he sneaked into my sleeping chamber like a thief? He was searching the room for something.

Yes, I knew. A portion of my consciousness let me on to it, like a thin, quaky treble of a whisper. How thankful I was that the veil of dark hid my face from his groping eyes in that moment.

But I would not say the word to myself inside my head, and I struggled under the onslaught of the realization to block out any thoughts regarding the shape of the thing this Formorrid was looking for.

Now his head turned toward me slowly, leaning out remarkably from between its shoulders. It was listening intently. Remembering what Alaric had told me about the mage skill of the Formorrid, and how it was rumored they could even read minds, I closed my eyes, wishing away the tiniest tendril of thought about the…

The scaly thing moved toward the door with fascinating stealth, held there for a few moments and disappeared through the narrow slit between door and jamb, shutting it behind him without the barest creak.

I let go of my breath in a swelling tide of relief and let the dreaded word form in my head: Lifenstone.

As soon as I had freshened up in the morning, Alaric was knocking on my door.

He began talking as soon as he stepped into my room. "Mead Moon is two weeks away, the month that yields the moon of marriage," he said. "I made sure Kilawey gets the news and several others kingdoms as well." After a pause, he said, "Frankly, I'm not sure we can expect anyone from Eirlandia. At least we can be on record to say we tried. My father's sending another ship, and it should arrive tomorrow."

"Your ladies will not be imprisoned in the hold this time," he added. I frowned at his jesting tone, and he wiped the smile off his face.

"Ahem, yes, well, anyway…" he seemed to lose his train of thought. "I will see you at Day meal?" That the last was a question not a statement made me realize he knew I was upset.

The Formorrid lurked in my thoughts. "Please send Briggiana in and I will give her the orders for others," I said. "I will be glad to continue our voyage. There's a strange malignancy in the air of this place. I want the wind of the open sea once again."

Alaric nodded and left and a little while later my Chief Lady-in-Waiting entered. I told her which of my things should be put in my cabin and what could be sent on the second ship.

After she had gone I walked to the window and opened the shutters. The day appeared cloudless, but there was a strange haze about. My necklace seemed heavier than usual. Sitting down on the window seat, I took out the stone.

"What is going on?" I whispered in Eirl.

I had found out that first night that the Lifenstone only responded to questions in that language.

No vision appeared this time to my question, but a small voice, I believe that of my mother's, answered inside my head:

The Formorrid are moving. Borrmid is a Great Worker, and he senses the Lifenstone, although he does not recognize it for what it is.

Still, he knows that Sidheran mage-power is at work in this part of the Dun, so he is trying to find it. Do not use this stone again until you are out at sea at least one full sun-time, so that you are beyond his range of knowing. The Formorrid are formidable, and he could cause you and yours much harm if he decided you were a threat. You must reach Vikland safely and be hand-fasted according to the rites of Alaric's people. Then you must find a way to return to Eirlandia and take up your rightful role as BanRighian of Kilbrae. In time, you will have an even greater destiny to fulfill, but you cannot do that until you have much more training; training which can only be completed in Eirlandia.

I put the necklace out of sight once more. Alaric had never asked me about the stone. I am pretty sure he did not know about its powers. Even I did not know the extent of its power at this point. I mentally imagined pulling a curtain between my thoughts and that of Borrmid.

"You shall not pass this boundary," I whispered to myself in Eirl.

All at once the heavy feeling lifted from me. Somehow my words had become reality, and Borrmid would not be able to track my movements and attempt to somehow shackle me with his magic any more.

The candle showed only a few moments left until the day meal. Not wanting to arouse any suspicion with Alaric, I hurried down the corridor to the main hall.

The next day when Vilk brought in my breakfast, it was obvious he was somewhat nervous.

"What is wrong, Vilk?" I asked. "What's going on?"

"I was instructed to tell you to stay out of the main hall until the ship captains from Vikland have conferred with Alaric. The emissary, Borrmid will be attending the meeting. Alaric told me he could not understand the Emissary's concern regarding your presence in the Dun. But he wanted to avoid you coming face to face with Borrmid by mistake."

I realized at once that Borrmid must be trying to access information about me but his questions would not have been explicitly directed at what he had come to seek while I slept.

"Alaric told me he had assured Borrmid that he hadn't observed anything about me that might drastically oppose the ordinary." Vilk sniffed, then continued, "It seemed that nothing Alaric said would get Borrmid out of his snit. So Alaric decided that it best Borrmid not lay eyes on you before we depart this place."

"The meeting could take some time." He told me. "Once the Emissary decides to leave, the captains and Alaric will have much to discuss." He put the tray down, saying, "I was told to bring you this meal and ask if you needed anything else."

I silently thanked my mother for her warning. Borrmid had, indeed, felt the power of the Lifenstone. He either wanted it for himself or wanted to destroy it.

"Thank you for breakfast, Vilk. I don't need anything. I will probably take a walk after breakfast, but I will be sure to stay close to my quarters."

Vilk nodded and headed out the door. I turned my attention on the tray and made short work of the light meal.

Afterward, I decided to walk between the scents in the garden. The land of the Vikes was much colder, and the blush of flora starkly different. While not exactly Vikland, I had been able to establish during my time in the Dun that it was located far enough north to have climate and flora more like Vikland than Eirlandia. Looking around at the brightly colored, fragrant climbers, I could spot the differences immediately. The blooming plants reminded me most of the snow flowers that grew in the few high ranges of my homeland. Delicate in looks, but hardy enough to withstand cold and harsh storms, these flowers were bright spots in a still mostly withered landscape. I brought a few flowers back into my room and placed the petals in my trunk around and under things, hoping their fragrance would linger awhile.

Before much more time had passed Vilk brought word that Borrmid had walked away in apparent disgust from the meeting and that Alaric wished to present me to his captains.

"I am only dressed informally," I told Vilk. "I hope Alaric understands that." Vilk assured me he did, and escorted me into the hall.

Alaric stopped conversing with a tall, bear-like man when he saw me. He guided me to the table laden with food and motioned to the other men to join him. Sven stood close to him in surprisingly courtly attire, while the servants poured us our meads.

Alaric raised his goblet and toasted to me, the mission, and the Great Ones. He gulped his mead and the others shouted: "Skool," before drinking deeply. A humble sip of the mead made me heady.

Alaric remained standing for his speech. "My captains, counselors, friends, I wish to present my soon-to-be Truwif, Tara of Kilbrae;

BanRigh, by blood, of that kingdom and as yet unconfirmed Tanista of Eirlandia. Twice of noble blood-her mother High Sidheran, her father Eirl of Ammerigan bloodline."

"All hail Prince Alaric and King Leeife," came Sven's cry. "All greetings to Truwif Tara of Kilbrae. May the Powers see you prosper."

The little mead I had taken was rushing to my head and I longed for food. As if hearing my thoughts, Alaric smiled and gestured to the waiting dishes.

"Eat now, my friends. Eat before this mead does its work too well and we cannot enjoy the food. Those who sail with me know their duties after this, as do those whose places will be here. Look to my good counselor, Sheifdar Sven for any last-minute advice. He sails but a day behind us, but his wisdom is yours for that one day, so use him well!" With that he sat down eagerly to eat.

"That idiot Borrmid showed up this morning before I ate," he whispered between morsels. "Since he refuses Vike food, I could only suffer in silence. I thought he would never go away. The questions he asked about you! Insufferable! Why he seems to think you are a threat, I can't begin to understand."

Little did I realize then, how right it was of Borrmid to have been nervous. In time, I would learn the Lifenstone's power, and my own.

"Do you think your people will accept me?" I asked softly, not wanting my neighbors to hear. "I don't want to spend my time watching my back for knives."

Alaric's eyes grew dark and his voice was cold, though soft. "We do not harm captives, and you will be special, since you will be a part of the royal family. No one would dare hurt you, and, really, they have no reason to. The Eirlandians are not our enemies, your people simply have things we want and need. It is a tradition in our land to take, not trade, unless taking is impossible.

"You are a high-ranking captive; you will be treated with the deference you deserve and are accustomed to. Vilk comes with us and has asked to be your personal body guard. If that suits you, I will let him know before we land. It means a promotion for him, so he will serve you loyally.

"Vilk was also a captive, once, but he embraced our ways. Most of our people accept him."

He wasn't angry at me for my question but I had a feeling he wasn't telling me everything.

"What is it like in Vikland?" I asked. "Are there law books available to me so I can further research and understand the ways and customs of your people?"

His eyes grew light and sparkled with humor. "My dear Tara, I want you to behave exactly as you would at home! I want my people to see how the women of Eirlandians behave. I don't think our laws are just in many cases, though please don't mention that to my father. Your people are right in giving women the same status in all things as men. I have seen your women fight, when they have to, just as well, or better, than their men. I know how shrewd they can be in bargaining, and how organized they need to be in running a household. I think some women would be better campaigners than men! Quartermaster would be a fine job for them. Even heading up a troop, if we could ever get the men to obey a woman's orders."

He smiled sheepishly. "We men will take some training and convincing. But I think seeing you, watching how you act and how decisive and bold and brave you are will do a lot toward convincing the Aalders that women have more talent, courage, and ability than we give them credit for."

I smiled at his enthusiasm but such a change would probably not happen until, and unless, he became king. He might, as Prince-Heir, get some beginning laws passed, but true equality would not come easily.

Even with laws written in the books, the outer settlements would take long years to adhere to the law. It was the same in Eirlandian, how could I expect different in Vikland?

At least in Eirlandian, we had a belief in deities where both the male and female were completely equal. In fact, if anything, the female was considered of slightly more importance, since it was the Mother Goddess who had created and nurtured the world at the beginning, and it was through her sufferance that any man partook of her bounty.

The wife had power over when crops would be planted, when animals would be sheared or slaughtered or even hunted. There were some high places with women judging and making our laws. They were less prone to bribes. Plus you couldn't ignore the receptive talent to sniff who was telling the true side of the story in a court of law.

The best I could achieve was stand behind Alaric's dream. His mead gone, he wiped his mouth and stood. "Lady Tara, Vilk will accompany you to the ship as soon as it's ready. We depart on the evening tide." He abruptly strode out of the room. None of the men present seemed confused, but I was stunned. I'd truly thought we were going the next day. Vilk appeared at my side and silently pulled back my chair. I rose and, to my astonishment, so did the men. I smiled nonplussed and nodded.

I smiled warmly at Sven and hoped he would not be long delayed in joining us. I considered him a friend and ally, and anyone like that should be where I could find them on first landing in Vikland.

For now, Alaric's absence had given me the perfect excuse to be alone. My necklace had grown heavy again and it was a sign it had something to communicate. I was desperate to get back to my room so I thanked the gentlemen for their company and turned to Vilk.

"Would you go check on how the packing's going? Do return in one candle mark," I said and he raised his eyebrows. He could find out about the packing and be back much sooner.

Back in my room, I locked the door so that none of my maids could come in unannounced, and sat down near the window overlooking the garden. When I took out the Lifenstone it pulsated with warmth.

I closed my eyes and whispered in Eirl, "Tell me what I need to know." As soon as the words had left my lips, everything went dark.

Chapter 6

The knocking on my door grew louder, indicating it had been persistent for some time.

"Lady Tara," Vilk's voice called from the other side. "Lady, are you alright? Can you hear me?" I realized my blackout must have lasted longer than I had thought.

"Yes, Vilk, I'm fine," I replied, standing and crossing to the door to unlock it. "I apologize, I must have dozed off," I explained as I let him in.

He scrutinized me with a sharp gaze, seemingly reading something in my eyes. "Well, Lady, I hope you enjoyed your nap," he said quietly. "All is prepared, and we must meet Alaric shortly to board the ship. I suggest you freshen up a bit and meet us in the Great Hall in one candle mark. I'll attend to some last-minute matters myself and join you there."

I nodded and turned towards the wash basin. Looking at my reflection in the mirror, I noticed slight lines of fatigue. The knowledge imparted by the Lifenstone lay deep within me for now. I knew I possessed more knowledge than before, but recalling it posed a danger in my current situation, so I let it remain dormant, trusting it would resurface when necessary.

I remembered, too, the warning of my mother from before regarding writing down this knowledge. Part of me knew that, sometime in the far future, my words would be read, but I had no idea by whom, and I could and would not let this knowledge be used by an enemy.

I washed my face and applied powder to diminish the appearance of fatigue. Then I tied my hair up and donned my cloak, the same sturdy one I wore upon my arrival. Alaric had told me it was "special" and provided protection against various dangers, including adverse weather conditions. I had a feeling there was more to the cloak than met the eye, as my necklace tingled slightly upon wearing it, as if acknowledging a kindred power.

I met Vilk in the Main Chamber as requested, and he guided me to a small antechamber where Alaric and Sven were engrossed in a discussion, a map spread out before them.

Upon seeing me, Sven's face lit up with a broad smile, and he swiftly rolled up the map. "Ah, Tara, it's good to see you again. I won't see you until after you're settled in the palace. I wanted to wish you a safe voyage." He approached me and embraced me warmly, like an uncle would his young niece. "You'll make a splendid Truwif to Alaric and a remarkable consort when the time comes. I believe Vikland will embrace you, and you, in turn, will find your place there after a period of adjustment for both of you." He grinned, as if sharing a private joke, then turned to Alaric.

"I'll leave you now, Cousin, to embark on your ships. I'll take care of things here and depart on tomorrow's tide. We shall meet again in Vikland, beneath the watchful gaze of the Father's Eye."

With a final embrace, Sven swiftly left the room, clutching the charts tightly in his hand.

Alaric gazed after his cousin for a moment, then seemed to collect himself. "Well, my lady," he addressed me. "It appears you are ready. As am I, and so are the ships. Let us bid farewell to this place and make our way back home."

"Head to your home, Alaric," I corrected him gently. "I have already left mine, and I suspect it will be some time before I return." Yet, I smiled as I spoke, ensuring my words carried no bitterness. This was my destiny, as my stone had foretold, and I was prepared to embrace it.

A slight smile formed on Alaric's lips as he offered his arm to me. Together, we traversed the Dun, taking a different route to avoid the Formorrid section of the fortress. I was grateful for that, eager to leave this place as swiftly as possible and avoid any encounters with Emissary Borrmid.

Opening a grand door, we stepped out onto the quay. Five imposing ships floated at anchor, and Alaric led me towards the largest one, adorned with a carved wolf's head at the bow. "This is my personal ship, The Wolfengaard. She has served me well, and now she will transport the greatest prize I've ever acquired... you." His eyes held a mixture of longing and pride as he looked at me. "I came to capture a princess, but it seems you have captured me instead. Come, I'll show you to your chambers." And so, I followed him up the gangplank, stepping into a new chapter of my life.

Chapter 7

While nothing much occurred during this leg of our journey to Vikland, there is something that bears writing about. Through the weeks at the Dun, I had realized more and more that my feelings for Alaric were turning from anger and resentment into softer feeling of actual warmth, friendship and even something more. It wasn't long after leaving the Dun that these feelings took a sudden turn.

I was standing on the deck of the ship when Alaric had come up behind me and lightly laid his hands on my shoulders. Turning, I looked up and him and beheld a passion in his eyes I had not seen before. It was not lust, but something deeper, and I realized I could see my own eyes mirrored in his and that they, too, held a passion I did not know existed.

"Alaric," I whispered, "What is going on?"

"My Eaglet," he breathed, "I had a dream last night. I think it was your Awen speaking to me. We were standing on a high hill looking at a strange city I had never seen before but somehow knew it was your home. You held a jewel in your hand, one I had never seen before, and it pulsed as if it were a heart."

"My home? Eirlandia? What city?"

Alaric reached for my hands and held them together in his. "I don't know the city, but I knew it was Eirlandia, I think its capitol? I only know a feminine voice whispered that it held the key to the future. The voice also said that both of us would be needed to keep that future safe."

"Oh, Alaric, I don't know what to say, or think about this," I replied. In my mind, I suddenly beheld the image of what he spoke. The city I beheld was indeed our capitol, specifically, it was the Nementon, the residence of the ArdRigh.

Alaric sighed softly. "Then say nothing," he whispered. He closed his eyes as he bent toward me. His lips touched mine, tentatively at first, then slightly stronger.

Suddenly, the Lifenstone warmed against my chest. Light headed, I gasped as my passions kindled. Letting my arms weave around him, I kissed him back with a passion stronger than his. He stiffened in surprise, soon surrendering to a frenzy of kisses and caresses.

Only when he undid the stays of my overdress and began to kiss my nipples that I put my hands out.

"No, Alaric, not here. At least let us have a bit of privacy. The weather is still a bit cold for a romp in the outdoors. Besides, I have no wish to be found in a compromising situation." I smiled to take the sting from my words, and gently rearranged my overdress. I stood, and took his hand. "Come," I said, "I know where we can go and not be disturbed."

As if under a spell, Alaric followed me to an unused room. Taking the key from the ring I always kept with me, I unlocked the chamber door and let him in. There was a slight chill in the room, but it was better than outdoors. The bed was made, so Alaric took an extra few covers from the chest at the foot of the bed and placed one on top.

"One cover is easier to wash in secret than a whole bed," he said.

I stood on one side of the bed, unsure. Part of my mind screamed this was wrong, but another part, louder, knew that this was actually completely right. Perhaps it was the influence of the Lifenstone, or maybe some part of me just knew it was time for the next step. I cannot really say, but I looking back I do not regret my actions.

Before going further, I remember I slipped the Lifenstone off from around my neck. To his quizzical look I said, "This is an heirloom from my mother, I do not want the chain broken." He simply nodded. Jewelry was not something he was thinking of at the moment.

I took the lead and took off Alaric's outer tunic. He followed by divesting me of my overdress. Next came his under chamois and my inner shift. That left me dressed in trews and my everyday corset. He was in trews only, and his boots. I pushed him playfully down onto the bed and tugged off his boots. Slipping out of my foot coverings, I jumped up and bestrode him, as one might an antlerres.

I played with his chest hair as he undid my corset, freeing my breasts and teasing the nipples until they stood out plump and pink. I tried pinning his arms above his head so I could have some respite from his teasing, but he was too strong and pushed me backwards.

Having swiftly reversed our positions, with one hand he clasped my hands above my head, continuing to tease me with the other.

He took my nipples in his mouth and relentlessly tongued them. The heat in my loins mounted and I felt strange moisture down there. Moaning, I tried to break free to overcome this almost frightening feeling.

"Oh, ho, so that is how it is," Alaric whispered. He released me suddenly, and stripped off my corset and trews so swiftly I could not even protest. Then he reached down and took down his trews also.

My eyes widened. I hadn't planned on this. "Alaric, I don't think..."

He stopped my words with kisses. "It is alright, Little Eaglet," he murmured. "I will not push you. We have time, plenty of it." He then pulled his trews back up and handed me my clothes. "I will leave you to redress," he said, his voice hinted of regret and even sadness. "I will see you at supper." With that he made a short court bow and left, closing the door behind him.

I sat up and stared into space. What, exactly, had just happened? I had wanted him, badly, but I couldn't go through with it. I hoped I hadn't quashed our budding relationship. I was determined to try again. Perhaps it just hadn't been the right time.

Other than that one time, the Lifenstone remained silent, offering no warnings or impressions. I somehow knew that it wouldn't communicate with me in this place, perhaps unable to do so. Maybe we were too far from Eirlandia, its birthplace. Regardless of the reason, I found myself truly alone, an exile from my home and all that was familiar. Only my servants remained by my side.

Upon reaching Haernstad, the capital city of Vikland Alaric left the ship almost before it came to halt to confer with his father and the Aalders, those counsellors deemed the wisest and most trusted.

Vilk stayed onboard to assist me in disembarking and would accompany me to my chambers in the Holmstead, the palace.

Standing on the foredeck, I looked at this city that would now be my home and was struck with how different it seemed. Built mostly of a gray stone, wooden boardwalks ran from the pier to what appeared to be the main street, where they split off to continue in front of building that appeared to be both shops and living quarters. Most were two stories high, the second story having many balconies on which hung clotheslines or small containers full of various growing plants, most of which I could not identify.

Livestock was being driven down the main street, along with people pulling or pushing carts loaded with produce and made goods and clothing.

As befitted the colder clime, the inhabitants wore fur-lined cloaks or coats. The women wore hats, many of them, but the men went hatless, their longer hair mostly tied back or braided. Almost all had tattoos on their arms and sometimes even their face, and most men did not wear shirts with sleeves, but instead sported laced vests made from animal skin. Their bare arms were tanned and many had a gold band on their forearm, most bearing some sort of mark I assumed might be a family or tribal emblem.

Pots of what would be blooming flowers in a couple more weeks, hung from posts set at intervals of ten feet. Lanterns, unlit at the moment, graced every doorway and often blank walls between doors. It was obvious the area would be well lit come nightfall.

Hearing a soft laugh, I turned to see Vilk standing beside a wheeled cart that was covered overhead by tanned hides, but open on the sides.

About six seats were fastened to the inside of the cart. A strong-looking black horse was in harness, with a driver, well wrapped up for the cold, on the front area.

"Come, Tanista," said Vilk, "Let's not gawk too long. The people here are not very tolerant of that sort of thing. The carriage will take you, myself and two guards to the palace. The pace will be slow enough for you to get a sense of the city without making a spectacle of yourself, which would make Alaric quite cross if he got wind on it."

Smiling sheepishly, I boarded the carriage, with Vilk beside and the two guards taking up positions before and behind us, both looking outwards. Their weapons were sheathed, but they definitely exuded an aura of quiet strength and lethal energy.

As we traveled away from the docks, the buildings changed from commercial and residential mixed to strictly residential. It was obvious we were entering the part of the city where the wealthier inhabitants lived. The houses were still about two stories, but they were a mixture of stone with wooden decorations, often painted with elaborate symbols and designs that were affixed to the walls, over doors and windows. Most of the second stories also boasted balconies, but these had ironwork and only flowerpots were handing from the railings. Often small tables and simple chairs were also in evidence.

The sun, surprisingly, was brightly shining, and as we appeared to approach an even larger building, which I assumed was the palace, I began to hear birds singing, and saw that the last hundred feet or so of the road was lined with tall pine trees. Peering ahead, I saw that what I assumed was a building was actually a very high wall with watch towers built every hundred feet or so. Guards stood watch at the top of these towers, and the walls themselves had small windows which, I had learned, were manned with skilled archers.

The wall was broken by a massive gate made from very thick wood and reinforced with iron bands. The gate stood open, and four guardsmen kept a close eye on everyone entering and leaving the palace.

Vilk reached out his hand, which held a scroll, as we approached, and the guards waved us forward without a word. We passed through an archway and into a courtyard that was nothing like I had ever seen.

The stone here was almost blindingly white in the sun. Ivy and holly and other evergreen plants grew against all the walls. A large statue, depicting a one-eyed man holding a book with one hand and staff with other dominated the middle of the courtyard. Two ravens sat on his shoulders, and I instinctively knew this was a depiction of a god, not a mortal.

Seeing my gaze, Vilk whispered in my ear. "That's Woodooen, the patron of the King's family. It is not wise to stare."

Blinking, I lowered my gaze and followed Vilk inside, where he quickly led me to my quarters.

My suites boasted exquisite furnishings and generous appointments.

My ladies had their own chambers, with one adjoining mine where a personal maid would sleep. The concept of having a personal maid was new to me, but Vilk explained that one had been assigned to me.

"We have many other Eirlandian captives from past raids," he informed me. "Usually, these are girls who caught the eyes of the men during the raids. They are brought back as house slaves but are treated more like servants. After seven years, they can earn income and buy their freedom. However, they are never allowed to return to their own country, as they might possess secrets that the Vikes prefer not to be divulged."

I nodded, familiar with this custom in other lands, though foreign to Eirlandia. "Your maid will also assist you in becoming more proficient in our language. I'm sure you have some knowledge, but most of our people don't speak Eirlandian unless they are traders, statesmen, or high-ranking raiders. Many at court have a basic understanding, but the sooner you learn Vike, the quicker you'll be accepted."

I smiled and nodded, choosing not to disclose the extent of my Vike language skills. That would remain my secret, at least for now. People tend to speak more freely when they believe they can't be understood, and I saw it as an advantage. Such knowledge would prove invaluable in the future, I was certain.

As if on cue, a timid knock sounded at the main chamber door. Vilk answered, stepping back to reveal a young girl in her late teens. Her red hair and green eyes immediately betrayed her Eirlandian heritage. "Sunshine on your head, Mistress Tara," she greeted me in Eirlandian. "I am Briggent, and I have been assigned as your personal maid."

"May the wind be soft and the sun warm," I responded formally. "Thank you, Briggent. Come in and commence your duties. My trunks are being transferred from the ship, but I assume some items are already here? A warm bath would be most welcome."

Briggent smiled. "Of course, my Lady. I have prepared one for you. This way, please." She led me to the bathing area, and Vilk bid farewell before taking his leave.

The bathing area consisted of a large circular depression in the floor. It was filled already with water that was hot enough to cause steam to rise. Steps led down into the water, and the rim was lined with small seats. I calculated it would hold about eight bathers at once.

Briggent helped me out of my clothes and let me make my tentative way into the water. The temperature was pleasing, neither too hot nor too tepid. "How?" I asked.

Briggent giggled before answering. "They are really quite ingenious. They use hot water from springs that flow beneath the palace. They have pipes that add cold water as needed so that the water isn't too hot. The water is said to be healing, and is only used for bathing, not drinking or cooking. The Vike have some luxuries such as this that we Eirlandians do not enjoy. I guess it makes for, at least in part, the rougher parts of living here, like the weather and the short days in the Dark Time."

After an exceptionally pleasant bath, surpassing my expectations, I donned one of the gowns selected by Briggent and settled down with some tea and biscuits. The cuisine possessed a slightly different flavor compared to what I was accustomed to, but it still emanated a sense of comfort and familiarity. Curious, I asked Briggent what the tea was and how the biscuits were made.

"The tea is from a plant that grows here," she answered in Eirl. Starseed, they call it. It is said to be of great medicinal value for many different things. I know of no plant like it at home. The biscuits use flax flour and honey. It creates a different texture and taste, which you will get used to. Wheat does not grow well here, too cold, so other plants are used in its place.

Master Alaric is very anxious for you to become fluent in his language, so let us begin even as you refresh yourself."

Briggent wasted no time and immediately commenced my language lessons, using Vike names for the items she served. Not wanting to start from scratch, I informed her in Vike that I possessed rudimentary knowledge of the language, sufficient for casual conversation in a court setting. However, I would rely on her guidance for unfamiliar terms. I also requested her solemn promise not to disclose my language prowess without my consent.

"Of course, Mistress," she replied. "I am at your service. I consider myself fortunate to have been chosen to serve you, as do all the Eirlandians here. Although we are not ill-treated, it is not the same as home. You are a piece of home to us, just as we are to you, I suspect. The life of an exile can be arduous, and we are all exiles. I doubt you will ever set foot in Eirlandia again."

"We shall see," I responded. "I have reason to believe this place won't be my home for long in the grand scheme of my life. I trust in the will of the gods and the weavings of destiny."

I spent the following hours acquainting myself with my new surroundings and the individuals who would serve me. Vilk acted as the head of my guard and personal protector, but there were also other maids, manservants, gardeners, laundresses, and even a designated groom to tend to any horses I might choose for my personal stable. I was being treated as a Ban-Righ and a Vikland Princess. This realization only intensified my sense of exile.

Approximately an hour before sunset, Alaric paid me a visit. He appraised my chambers with a critical eye, seemingly satisfied with what he observed.

"So, my dear Tara, are these chambers to your liking? Have you met your staff? This section of the Holmstead has been designed to evoke the essence of Eirlandia, to the best of my abilities. You are an unofficial envoy of Eirlandia, you know, being the first noble to set foot in Vikland. The court is abuzz with excitement over your arrival."

"That reminds me," he continued, a mischievous twinkle in his eyes. "We are to dine with my father and his inner court tonight. A reception is planned in your honor. Following the handfasting, you will be introduced to the full court during the festivities."

"Technically, I'm not supposed to see you after tonight until our handfasting in a week or so. However, I convinced my father and the Aalders that this is not a typical state marriage. You need someone who can speak both Eirlandian and Vike to help you during this transitional period. Therefore, I can see you, accompanied, as necessary for state affairs until the morning of the handfasting. I know your maid has been giving you lessons, but there are things regarding statecraft that she does not know. You will continue with her also, I will only step in if it seems you are unsure of something."

"What about the handfasting?" I inquired.

"I will provide more details about your role in the ceremony later. For now, I wanted to inform you that all your belongings have arrived at the palace and are being transported here. I would like you to wear the gown I had you wear when we encountered the Formorrid. It has been set aside and should be in your maid's quarters by now, properly prepared. The large cloak won't be required, but the dress holds great significance. It was the attire my mother wore during state occasions like tonight's presentation. By wearing it, I convey that I consider you equal to my mother—a genuine compliment."

I opened my mouth to inquire further, but the words failed to escape. I somehow knew it wasn't the appropriate time or place for extensive questioning.

"I appreciate the historical context of the gown," I responded. "I will wear it with pride. When should I expect you to collect me for dinner?"

"Will one candlemark be sufficient? That will allow me time to give you a brief tour and acquaint you with the individuals you will meet during the meal. It's essential to make a favorable impression. Well, except for the Formorrid. I still don't comprehend why they took a disliking to you..."

Alaric trailed off, seemingly waiting for a response. I remained silent. I knew precisely why the Formorrid hadn't warmed up to me, but I had no intention of delving into that topic now.

"Very well," he continued after a moment of silence, "I will come for you in one candlemark." At that moment, a gentle knock sounded at my door. "Ah, I bet that's your maid with the dress. Until then, my lady." He inclined his head, refraining from kissing my hand. Straightening himself, he opened the door. Indeed, Briggent stood outside, holding the dress. Alaric gestured for her to enter before swiftly departing, closing the door behind him.

Briggent glanced after him briefly, shaking her head, before approaching me. "This is the gown I was told you would wear tonight, my lady," she said, her voice tinged with surprise. "It isn't Eirlandian, but I was informed that no alterations were necessary since you had worn it before."

"That's correct, Briggent. I have worn it before. Please assist me in removing this dressing gown, and let's get into the dress. I only have one candlemark to prepare myself for meeting the King and his close advisors. I aim to exude regality and showcase my Eirlandian heritage as much as possible, despite the gown I must wear."

Without further delay, Briggent began unfastening the ties, initiating my transformation into the Eirlandian Ban-Righ that the court seemed to anticipate.

Chapter 8

The Great Hall of the Court of King Leeife of Vikland impressed me with its magnificent stone carvings and rich tapestries. The colors were rich and bold, and many of the scenes were of battles, dominated with reds and golds. Some others showed sea going ships with strange looking serpents seeming to sail alongside the vessels. The air was scented with pine and smell of warmed, mulled mead. The hall was comfortably warm, thanks to the large fire rings scattered throughout, though I was more accustomed to a milder climate.

Alaric nodded approvingly as he escorted me to the hall, but he had said nothing to prepare me for the upcoming audience. When pressed, he simply advised me to be myself and behave as I would have in my father's court. Filled with both anxiety and anticipation, I vowed to show these Vikes what true royalty looked like.

As we approached the front of the hall, my eyes fell upon a large throne on a raised platform. Beside it, a smaller throne stood, and two others were arranged on the lower level.

Seated upon the upper throne was King Leeife, a commanding figure in the prime of his life. His golden hair cascaded in braids down his chest, and a crown fashioned in the likeness of a wolf's head adorned his brow. He wore a robe made of white wolf fur, secured by elaborate gold chains. A ceremonial steel axe, edged with silver, leaned against the right side of his throne. He exuded regality, embodying the essence of a Vike king.

Alaric stepped forward, motioning for me to wait. With a salute, he addressed the king in a resounding voice, "All hail Mighty King Leeife! Behold, I present the Eirlandian BanRigh Tara, as you commanded. On the Eve of Freyatine, she shall be my Truwif, as per your decree. I bring her before you now to demonstrate my success." With that, he gestured for me to approach.

Taking two steps forward, I stood beside Alaric. I performed a curtsy befitting one ruler to another. If Alaric wished to address me as BanRigh, I would carry myself accordingly. A BanRigh recognizes no superior except the ArdRigh or ArdRighian, not even a ruler of another land.

As I completed my bow, I met Leeife's gaze and saw a mixture of amusement and approval in his eyes. However, from the corner of my eye, I caught glimpses of less welcoming expressions. Some directed dark looks in my direction.

"Prince Alaric," the King began, his voice carrying across the hall, "and BanRigh Tara, I extend a warm welcome to Haernstad. I hope your voyage was pleasant, and Lady Tara, I trust you shall find your stay with us both pleasant and fruitful."

A soft ripple of laughter spread through the room, suggesting a double entendre in his words.

"Only the High Ones know the future, Majesty," I replied. "I shall strive to ensure that the seeds of this adventure find fertile ground." Let them discover that Eirlandians are adept at employing double meanings as well.

Alaric suppressed a chuckle, disguising it as a cough. "My King, may we have permission to sit? The taste of my voyage still lingers, and I crave a sip of good Vikland mead to wash it away."

The King waved his hand in agreement, and we proceeded to the seats arranged just below his throne. I glanced at the empty seat beside the king, realizing that the Queen Consort was absent from tonight's gathering. Alaric noticed my gaze and whispered quietly, "There is currently no Queen Consort in Vikland. My mother has passed away, and my father has yet to remarry. I doubt he ever will, as he cherished my mother deeply."

"I'm sorry," I whispered back. "I understand the pain of growing up without a mother."

"Vikland is in need of the wisdom of a Great Mother now. I hope you can fulfill that role," Alaric said softly. "Observe and listen closely. I know you possess more knowledge of the Vike language than most believe. Let them continue in their assumption.

You are clever and intelligent. I need you to be my eyes and ears. My father and I have plans, but there are those who oppose us. In due time, we will confide in you. For now, represent your homeland and inform me of anything of interest that you may hear."

At that moment, a servant approached with mead, causing our conversation to pause. The musicians began to play, and court members gradually approached us, engaging Alaric in small talk.

As many believed I had little to no understanding of the Vike language, I would simply smile and converse with Alaric, who would play along with the ruse, translating their words into Eirlandian for me. He would also provide a brief overview of each person's court position when it was not readily apparent.

After what felt like an eternity, King Leeife rose from his throne and descended to our level. "Prince Alaric, I request the honor of dancing with your betrothed," he formally declared. The room stirred with anticipation, and I could hear rustling and gasps of surprise.

"Certainly, my King," Alaric replied, "if Lady Tara consents. Eirlandians are independent individuals, and she possesses some knowledge of the Vike language. You can ask her yourself."

His response caused even more commotion, but the King merely smiled and turned to me, raising an eyebrow in question.

"The King honors me," I replied in Vike. "I would be delighted to dance, although I am unfamiliar with the steps here."

The King chuckled. "They are easy, simply follow the others. They are not so different from some of your own dances, I presume."

And indeed, he was right. I found myself easily navigating the steps of several dances with the King before Alaric came to retrieve me. By that time, I was breathless and eagerly accepted a glass of mead, quickly downing it. I followed it with a cup of clear water, ensuring my senses remained sharp.

After the dancing concluded, a delectable feast was served. A table was brought before our seats, adorned with an array of dishes. The King had a large tray by his throne, while smaller tables mysteriously appeared around the room, drawing the courtiers towards them as if by magic.

Alaric noticed my confusion and smiled. "The tables are always present, concealed within the pillars," he explained. "Folding stools are brought out for the guests to sit on. The preparations took place while we were dancing. It gives the illusion of magic to those who are unaware, but it is mostly a matter of skillful coordination and meticulous planning." I nodded, taking in the spectacle, knowing that I would uncover many more secrets in due time.

During the meal, the musicians played softly, allowing for conversations to flow. As most guests finished their meals, small groups began to gather, some around tables where food still remained, but mostly in the spaces between the tables.

Alaric utilized this opportunity to point out various court members, their names, and titles. He assured me that I need not remember them all immediately, but the more familiar I became with their faces, the easier it would be to recall their identities.

A few more individuals approached the king and us, but for the most part, we were left undisturbed, though many curious gazes were cast our way. I wondered what they were thinking and how many of them I could classify as friends, foes, or neutrals.

A few individuals smiled at me, but the majority bore haughty expressions. A small group, positioned farthest away, appeared almost hostile, and I pondered the reason behind their animosity. Perhaps these were the ones who disapproved of Alaric marrying a foreign princess? In Eirlandia, we also had such individuals who believed that only those of pure Eirlandian blood were fit for the ruling class. I found the notion foolish; we were already closely related enough. Introducing fresh blood ensured that our offspring would be strong, and new ideas would continually be brought forth.

Once everyone finished their meal, the King called for the court's attention. In no time at all, the tables were cleared, and the courtiers settled into chairs arranged in orderly rows before the King and ourselves.

A vacant space was left at the front, indicating that entertainment was about to commence. The King announced that the Chief Skaald himself would perform that night, causing a murmur of anticipation to ripple through the crowd. It seemed to be a rare occurrence. I whispered the same sentiment to Alaric, who nodded in agreement.

"Skaald Odine rarely performs in public," Alaric informed me. "He is usually occupied with his duties. I believe Father asked him to perform tonight as a special honor to you. He has studied Eirlandian history and society extensively and has composed a lay in your honor."

"Truly?" I whispered. "I am eager to experience it."

Just then, silence enveloped the hall. To my left, I witnessed the Skaald's entrance through a small doorway hidden in the shadows. Had I not been intently observing that spot, it would have seemed as though he had materialized out of thin air, stepping from the shadows into the hall's illuminated space.

With a gesture, the lamps toward the back of the hall were extinguished, leaving only the front area, where we sat, bathed in light.

In this illumination, the Skaald's robe shimmered as if adorned with mica or some other precious material, capturing the flickering light. It was a splendid sight, regardless of the technique employed, and the performer within me, inherent to my Eirlandian nature, appreciated the showmanship.

Approaching the front, the Skaald bowed to the king and inclined his head towards us before turning to face the audience.

"Esteemed guests," he began, his voice rich and carrying effortlessly through the hall, despite not being excessively loud. "Tonight, at the behest of King Leeife, I come to honor our soon-to-be Princess. As you are aware, she hails from Eirlandia, and I have crafted a special lay in her honor. The Eirlandians are not our adversaries. Though we have conducted raids on their coasts and claimed slaves and treasures, they are far from weak or inferior in any way.

"This lay will illustrate their strength and noble nature, showcasing their unique way of thinking and living. They walk the path of peace whenever possible, yet they possess knowledge of war. They are not doves, but eagles. Listen and learn about this remarkable people." With a bow, he ascended to the same level as the King, where his voice would reach all in attendance.

Shifting slightly in my seat, I noticed him standing beside a grand harp. I was astounded. I had not realized that the Vikes had harpers among them. Harper-bards were rare even in Eirlandia, so encountering a Vike Skaald possessing such skill was truly remarkable. Still, I had yet to hear the man perform, and I wondered if he would merely pluck at the strings occasionally, like an apprentice bard, while primarily narrating his tale through words. I was sorely mistaken about the talent of Skaald Odine.

Attempting to recite the Lay of Eirlandia here would be futile, as it was far too intricate and lengthy. The musical composition and lyrics have been transcribed and included in the court records for anyone who wishes to read and attempt to perform this masterpiece.

To those who undertake such a feat, I wish you the best of luck and the guidance of the Mighty Ones, for only with their aid can justice be done to it.

Skaald Odine's skill was beyond extraordinary. His stature certainly belied his abilities. He appeared just past middle age, with hair the color of winter wheat, which hung to his shoulders, with a braid on each side framing his weather-worn face. I understood within a few moments that the braids were to keep his hair from his face as he bent over the harp strings. His build was slighter than most of his countrymen, but it seemed wiry, and I had no doubt he was stronger than he looked. His tunic was long, almost a robe, but his leggings showed from just below his needs until taken up by half boots that ended just above his ankles. The fabric was rich and soft looking, and the color was a deep purple. I would come to know that the color announced his rank as a High Skaald, akin to our ArdDrui.

His voice possessed a range and richness that I had only heard of in tales but never witnessed firsthand. His mastery of the harp ranked second only to the legendary Ammerigan from our country's ancient past.

Truly, he conveyed the history and grand achievements of my people flawlessly, captivating the audience with his consummate skill and showmanship. I was rendered speechless and found tears welling in my eyes as the piece concluded—a truly lengthy and awe-inspiring performance. Stealing a glance at Alaric beside me, I could see that he, too, appreciated the lay, although his emotional response was not as intense as mine.

Prompted by an indescribable sensation, akin to a command, I rose to my feet after the applause subsided, removing a small yet valuable pin that I had discovered among my jewelry earlier that afternoon. I had decided at the last moment to wear it.

Looking up and behind me at the maestro, I spoke aloud in resounding Vike, "Esteemed Master Skaald, I offer my gratitude. I possess little with which to reward you, but I beseech you to accept this modest gift, a token from the land you have so exquisitely extolled in your lay." Extending my hand, I awaited the Skaald's acceptance.

For a moment, he appeared taken aback, and I wondered if I had committed a breach of etiquette. However, the King and Alaric both smiled and nodded approvingly. Odine descended the steps, opening his hand to receive the gift. As I placed the pin in his palm, my Lifenstone warmed and reassured me. It became apparent to me that this Skaald would hold great importance in Vikland, and I sensed an instinctual alliance forming—a powerful ally indeed.

"BanRigh Tara," Odine proclaimed in resounding tones, slipping the pin onto his cloak, "I accept your gift with gratitude and hereby pledge, in the presence of this esteemed company, my unwavering support and friendship throughout your sojourn in our realm."

A barely audible gasp emanated from some in the hall, affirming my intuition that this man was a formidable ally and, potentially, a friend. With that, the Skaald bowed once more to the King, then to Alaric and myself, before departing the hall.

The lower part of the hall was illuminated once again, and the King ordered more wine to be served. As we indulged in conversation and drink, a troupe of acrobatic dancers took the stage. The remainder of the evening was filled with light entertainment, vibrant discussions, and merriment.

As the night grew late, I found myself growing drowsy.

Suddenly, the King stood, and silence befell the room. "I shall retire now," he declared. "Likewise, my family shall do the same. If you wish to remain, please do so. Our new family member is weary from her journey and in need of rest."

With that, he approached Alaric and me, extending his arm to me. I smiled and took it, walking with him on my left and Alaric on my right, down the hall and out the door, all the while sensing eyes upon us—thoughtful, angry, hopeful, amazed. My first official day had concluded, and many more lay ahead.

Chapter 9

I have spoken of the fact the Lifenstone remained quiet during my time in Vikland, so I don't quite understand something that happened one day about a week after my arrival in Vikland.

Alaric and I saw little of each other outside of court appearances and dinner, but there was one afternoon when we somehow managed to be in the same place at the same time. Perhaps it was the setting of the quiet solarium, a room I had discovered quite by accident a few days before, and one I had taken to returning to whenever I could. The room boasted a small fountain, and was filled with lovely, fragrant flowers. Cushioned benches dotted the room, each one within its own bower of flowers and completely private.

I was sitting in one of those private spaces meditating, when I heard the sound of another person entering the room. I stood up and walked to the entrance. Just turning a corner was none other than Alaric, informally dressed, just as I was, in simple trews and a shirt. I wore only a female version of the same outfit, having forgone even a light corset, as I had felt somewhat flushed after the wine I had drunk during midmeal.

Seeing me, Alaric grinned broadly and silently gestured if he might approach. Smiling widely, I nodded and gestured him to come inside.

"I was not expecting to find you here," Alaric greeted me, keeping his voice soft, even though we were alone. "I had no idea you had found this old solarium. I thought I was the only one who came here anymore."

Sitting down on the coach I had vacated moments before; I gestured for him to sit beside me. "Why is that?" I asked.

"This was my mother's favorite room in the Homestead," he answered, his voice filled with remembrance and longing. "You could find her here if she was not in court or her rooms. She and left strict instructions that the room was always to be cared for and kept neat and clean even if she was not around, for she knew how I also loved the place."

My face must have reflected my sorrow for him, I had not forgotten the deaths of my own father and brother, although it some ways it seemed almost a lifetime ago.

"It is alright, Little Eaglet," he said, calling me by the pet name he had adopted for me in the time after we left the Formorrid Dun. "Do not be sad for me. I know my mother watches over me, and I am sure she is pleased with my chosen mate."

"Truly?" I asked. "Do you think she would have accepted me, were she still alive?"

"Has my father not accepted you?" he countered. "I believe he has, for he does little but sing your praises to all who will listen."

I blushed a bit then. Looking at him, it seemed I could almost see his Anima, his soul light, forming a nimbus around him. He looked almost other-worldly, a bit like Lugh in his eyes and smiling face.

I reached out and touch his cheek. His eyes widened and he gently put his arm around me and drew me closer.

"What is this, my Tara?" he asked. "Have you decided it is time?"

"I don't know," I answered truthfully. "I was taught that our class does not engage in intimate behavior before we are joined in the sight of the gods. And we are not joined in such a way, not yet."

"How does one do this joining in Eirlandia?" he asked.

"It can be a private thing," I answered. "Usually the betrothed couple goes to the sacred grove, or other sacred space. There they proclaim their love before the gods and vow to each other that their gift of their bodies, mind and anima, which you call spirit, is given freely and in love."

Alaric grinned with delight at these words, and a somewhat mischievous twinkle happened in his eyes.

"Then let us join in your way, before we do so in mine," he proposed.

"I am not ready for body-joining," I warned. "But I am happy to be joined. We can wait for a more appropriate time and place for my nighting."

His smiled slipped a little, but he nodded. "Agreed. I told you once before I would wait until we are hand-fasted, and that is very soon. I can be patient."

"Alright then," I stood up and took his hand. "Let us go to the fountain. The space is clear and the water is a symbol of renewal and new life. With our vows we are agreeing to a new life together, a new portion of our life journey is about to begin."

We walked together, hand in hand, to the central fountain. The room was utterly silent except for the sound of the fountain and our own breathing.

I turned to Alaric and gazed into his eyes, "I, Tara, do give to you, Alaric, my whole self. I gift you my love, respect, companionship and support. I give this with all love and declare before all the gods and Old Ones that I give this freely. With this kiss do I seal this vow," and I kissed him, a kiss that held all my passion, hopes, fears and joys. I don't know if it lasted seconds or minutes, but I was filled at that moment with a complete sense of rightfulness and fulfillment and approval from the Old Ones and Guardians.

"Now you," I murmured after the kiss had ended and I caught my breath.

Taking a deep breath, Alaric repeated the vow. "I, Alaric, do give to you, Tara, my whole self. I gift you my love, respect, companionship and support. I give this with all love and declare before all the gods and Old Ones that I give this freely. With this kiss do I seal this vow," and he kissed me with the same intensity and passion. What he felt I cannot say, but I knew, of a certain, that my gods were with us at the moment and that they gave us our blessing. In their sight we were truly joined, and whatever happened afterwards with the formal handfasting was just for show.

We walked to the doorway together, but Alaric dropped my hand and silently signaled me to wait a few moments. Then he slipped through the door and was gone. I did not see him until the next day.

The next few days were ordinary in many ways, but they were filled with anticipation as the handfasting was scheduled for the next full moon, which was only five days away.

I vividly recall that the day dawned brightly, devoid of any hint of a storm. As was my custom, I awoke early and enjoyed a light breakfast. The ceremony was scheduled for High Sun, followed by an elaborate feast and celebration. Although the ceremony itself would be relatively intimate, with only select members of the court in attendance and the Chief Skaald presiding, I felt relieved by the smaller gathering. I possessed enough knowledge of Vike to understand the proceedings, and I didn't want to be distracted by a large crowd during such a momentous occasion, already fraught with nervousness surrounding marriage.

Briggent entered shortly after I finished my meal and escorted me to the awaiting bath. Once prepared, oiled, and perfumed, I was dressed in multiple layers of clothing, each with specific cultural significance, which I won't attempt to delve into here. Suffice it to say that the bride is enveloped in protective magic on her handfasting day, as it was believed that the Aellfa, the demon folk of the frigid lands, sought opportunities to afflict the new bride with coldness and infertility. As we no such belief in Eirlandia, I was relieved when Briggent and told me all about the dressing ceremony, and assumed magic of the garments. She had done this before I retired the night prior, regaling me with stories from Vike folklore regarding the Aellfa and their tricks. These demons were very unlike even our worse trouble makers, such as pixies and gnomes, who could play harmless tricks and jokes, but who never truly harmed their victims.

Finally, dressed in a gown adorned with white and gold, my Lifenstone concealed beneath the layers, and a magnificent diamond necklace adorning my throat, I slipped into my slippers and made my way to the window of my chambers. There, I offered a silent prayer to my own deities, seeking their blessings, protection, and guidance during my time in this unfamiliar land. I also prayed for the safety and well-being of my father's tribe, now without a ruler. I knew, of course, that by now the Elders had most likely found a new Righ, or, at the least, the ArdRigh had appointed someone to temporarily take over the duties of the Righ until a formal council could elect a new one. I had a few cousins who would be in line, and I hoped that one of them would take up the torc of kingship.

A knock on the door interrupted my thoughts, and Briggent answered it. To my surprise, it was not Vilk, whom I had expected, but Sven, radiating regal elegance like never before.

"Greetings and blessings on this fair day to the loveliest of brides," Sven greeted, bowing low. "Since you lack a male relative to accompany you, I beseeched and was granted the honor of being your champion during this time."

I returned the bow. "I am truly pleased and grateful, Sven. I consider you a dear friend, and I am overjoyed to see you once more." Indeed, I hadn't seen him since my departure from the Formorrid Dun.

"Are you ready?" he asked. I nodded, taking his arm as he escorted me through a part of the homestead I had yet to explore. Eventually, we arrived at a breathtaking location—an expansive courtyard overlooking a vast bay, known as a fjord. To the right, a towering snow-capped mountain captivated my gaze. I had never witnessed a mountain of such magnitude. Near its peak, a sizable opening was apparent, seemingly drilled through the mountain, allowing the sun to shine through at specific hours or on certain days. I stood frozen, my Lifenstone aglow, not in warning but in recognition of this majestic sight.

"Behold the Father's Eye," Sven whispered softly. "The sun illuminates it precisely at the summer solstice, which occurs tomorrow."

He smiled gently. "Come, they are waiting. The ceremony is brief, and soon you shall be reunited with Alaric."

With those words, he guided me across the courtyard, passing through an unnoticed gate. Beyond it lay a bower adorned with white flowers, leading to a grotto where Skaald Odine stood, beckoning me forward. As I took a step, the sweet melodies of hidden musicians filled the air. The music bore a certain familiarity, though it was not Eirlandian, containing elements that interwove with my native tunes. I passed by a few familiar faces from the court presentation and found myself standing before the Skaald.

From the corner of my eye, I noticed Sven stepping back, and I sensed another presence on my left. Yet my gaze remained fixed on the Skaald, who stood before me in quiet contemplation, his gaze locked with mine. As the music ceased, the Skaald's voice resounded.

"Prince Alaric, BanRigh Tara," the Skaald intoned, "you come together on this day to be united before this esteemed gathering, in the presence of the gods, and beneath the gaze of the Father's Eye. BanRigh Tara, as a foreigner to our land, you may pose any question you desire without it being construed as an offense to our gods or our people. Do you have a question?"

I shook my head. In the past few days, I had received thorough instruction on what to expect and the history and significance of the ritual. Although somewhat different from our customs, the Vikland handfasting ceremony held familiar elements and shared the same purpose.

Skaald Odine nodded and produced a cord, proceeding to bind our arms together with it.

"As this cord now binds you," he declared, "remember that you are bound before the people and the gods, from this day forward, regardless of any physical distance that may separate you. The words you are about to speak shall unite your lives and souls until the gods decree otherwise. Be aware and remember this, for the knot tied today can never truly be severed except by the will of the gods. Prince Alaric, please state your intentions."

"I, Prince Alaric Leifson of Vikland, come forth on this day to be handfasted with Tanista Tara Eduardotterson of Eirlandia," Alaric proclaimed with strength and pride. "I declare her my Truwif, granting her all the rights, protection, privileges, and duties of that position. I offer her my strength, my championship, my honor, and my love for as long as the gods decree."

Though Alaric's voice wasn't particularly loud, it carried clearly to all present. A small gasp rippled through the audience at his declaration of love, indicating that this sentiment may not have been a customary part of the ceremony. Given that many political marriages lacked genuine affection, especially in the beginning, this unexpected proclamation seemed logical.

"Tanista Tara, having indicated your understanding of the rite, I now ask you to state your intention," the Skaald prompted.

The gathered onlookers audibly gasped as I spoke, answering in flawless Vike, my words echoing through the air.

"I, Tanista Tara Eduardotterson of Eirlandia, come forth on this day to be handfasted, of my own will and desire, to Prince Alaric Leifson of Vikland. I acknowledge my rank as Truwif, along with the rights, protection, privileges, and duties that accompany such a title. For my part, I bestow upon Alaric my honor, my Self, and my love for as long as the gods decree.

"I also declare that, should we ever return to my homeland, I will defend Prince Alaric as my true consort before the Eirlandians."

The sharp intake of breath, including Alaric's, indicated that my proclamation had caught everyone off guard. Only the Skaald seemed unsurprised, smiling slightly and inclining his head, as if expressing agreement or support.

"Alaric and Tara," Odine announced, "you have declared your intent and have been bound in the presence of the gods and your people. Now, pull the cords and tie the marriage knot for all to witness. May the gods of both Vikland and Eirlandia bless your union."

Following his instructions, we pulled our arms back, creating a knot in the cord that had bound us together. Turning, we held the knotted cord high for all to see. "Welcome, then, to the new couple! Welcome the Prince and Princess of Vikland! Skool!"

"Skool!" the crowd resounded. "Blessings upon the couple!" The king stepped forward, presenting us with matching rings. We exchanged the rings, then handed the cord to a waiting servant. It would be sealed in a box and stored away, hopefully never to be brought out again until our deaths, when the surviving partner could choose to untie the knot, symbolizing the end of the bond. Occasionally, the survivor would leave the knot intact, signifying a refusal to remarry.

With that final ritual completed, Alaric and I proceeded down the aisle and entered the vast area where I had first beheld the Father's Eye. Now, it teemed with people, tables, chairs, food, mead, and music. I confess to having a few goblets of strong mead, and I can honestly recall very little of the ensuing festivities, which continued until the sun hung low on the horizon and exhaustion claimed me. At that point, Alaric rose, announced our departure, and whisked me away.

However, we didn't return to either of our chambers. Instead, he led me to a carriage and assisted me inside.

"Rest a while, my dearest," he said. "We have a short journey ahead to the special wedlock house where we will spend the next few weeks. Sleep now, my love. It's all right. I understand. You are unaccustomed to our mead and have had a long day. Besides, there will be no true night for several months, so you may as well grow accustomed to it."

I was so fatigued that I simply nodded and closed my eyes, intending to rest and let the effects of the mead dissipate. However, I slept throughout the entire journey, awakening only when the carriage came to a halt and a flurry of activity ensued, indicating the unloading of trunks.

As I opened my eyes, I realized that Alaric was no longer within the carriage. Moments later, the door opened, and my husband extended his hand to help me step out.

"We have arrived, Beloved. Come, let us enter. Refreshments await." Nodding, and feeling an undeniable thirst, I took his hand and disembarked.

Dusk still enveloped the surroundings, and I recalled that the sun would not truly set for several months. This was the Season of Allday, the Time of Growing unique to these lands. Yet here I was, and I would need to accustom myself to counting time by candle marks rather than relying solely on the sun and natural light.

Crossing the threshold, I noticed the house servants eagerly awaiting our arrival. They were all strangers to me. In Vike, I greeted each one and accepted a glass of clear, cold liquid from the female servant.

"Clear water from the goddess' well," she informed me. "Drink and be sustained by Freyate, she of the waters and the land." Grateful for the offering of fresh spring water instead of more mead, I nodded my thanks and drank deeply.

Having quenched my thirst, I observed Alaric doing the same. "I have a need and a yearning that require solitude. Will you lead the way, my mate?"

With a glimmer in his eyes, he nodded and took my hand, guiding me swiftly down a hallway that culminated in an ornate door adorned with a beautiful bough of flowers.

"Enter now the sacred chambers of the Bonded Suite. This suite of rooms is reserved solely for newly hand-fasted couples. We shall have no reason to leave this abode during the entirety of our honeymoon, for it encompasses a garden and even a section of the forest should we desire to hunt or spend time alone in nature."

With that, he pulled me forward and ushered me inside, firmly closing the door behind him. What followed is a time that I will always remember and cherish, as it was the beginning of a lifetime of marital bliss.

Chapter 10

Maeve

Maeve closed her eyes, realizing she had spent more time reading than expected. She knew she should return the book promptly so the researchers could find the necessary information about the Crowns. However, she couldn't help but wonder about the Lifenstone Tara mentioned. Perhaps finding the stone first could expedite their search. She pondered if it might be in the library somewhere.

With a sense of purpose, Maeve marked her spot in the journal, wrapped it carefully, and placed it in her tote bag. She retraced her steps, but it was already night outside, so she settled in the library to prepare a meal and sleep.

The next morning, Maeve woke early and ate a quick meal. Although she wanted to know more of the Great ArdRighian's story, she reminded herself to reach the way- cabin first. As she journeyed, she reflected on the advancements in Eirlandia and Vikland over the centuries and the current unrest caused by the Formorrid. The task given to her was to find the original journal and the crowns for Tara's and Alaric's upcoming ceremony.

The way-cabin came into view sooner than expected, and Maeve decided to rest there and skip ahead in the journal to Tara's return to Eirlandia. She believed she would have valuable information for the scholars by the time she reached Kilawey.

After settling in the cabin, Maeve sat on the porch with the book, searching for a sentence that would guide her to the appropriate section. She skimmed through Tara's early months in Vikland, her friendship with Skaald Odine, and the intrigues of the court. But it was several chapters ahead where she found the mention of the Lifenstone and Eirlandia.

With daylight still remaining, Maeve settled into the chair and resumed reading.

Chapter 11

The days that followed were both full to the brim with happenings and routine at the same time. Through long conversations with King Leeife, we began to form a true bond of friendship and trust. I cannot in good conscience go into detail here about the conversations, but it soon became clear that Leeife considered me as part of the family, not just a captive for political reasons.

Leeife was aware that I could one day be named ruler of Eirlandia, and was already beginning to plan for negotiations between our two lands to begin. News had been sent, in my own hand, explaining my situation as wife of the Royal Prince and a member in full standing within the Vikland court. I asked in my correspondence that I be named an official ambassador to Vikland, which all the powers and responsibilities that appointment entailed.

We had yet to receive a reply, but it had not yet been long enough to assume the offer had been rebuffed. In anticipation of my appointment, King Leeife, Alaric and myself, along with Skaald Odine and a few other close advisors, spent hours formulating possible agreements and petitions to pave the way toward a lasting peace and mutually beneficial trade between our countries.

One morning, news reached the court that an unexpected messenger had arrived from Eirlandia, seeking an audience with King Alaric and me. It was surprising that the Eirlandians would send such a person. He claimed to be a Royal Bard under the protection of the ArdRigh of Eirlandia, and had arrived under a flag of truce. After being offered refreshment, he awaited our decision on whether to receive him.

Seated on our thrones, Alaric and I discussed the messenger's arrival. King Leeife, also present, dismissed the entire court except for the guards who were too far away to hear our conversation. We debated the authenticity and intentions of the messenger, considering the possibility of espionage or violence.

"No Eirlandian would claim the status of Royal Bard without being one," I stated. "The Bards are trained to memorize messages for times of war or negotiation, when a written message could be compromised."

"I've heard of this," Alaric said. "The Formorrid warned me to be cautious of strangers from Eirlandia, even captives, as they could be bard spies in disguise. They fear our alliance with Eirlandia and the potential discovery of Eirlandians with Sidheran heritage."

Acknowledging the concerns, King Leeife nodded. "Prince Alaric, please bring in the Counsels and see that this official messenger is brought before us with all speed. I have no reason to suspect he is different from what he claims. Our good Tara will, I'm sure, be able to vouch for his authenticity."

I nodded. I knew by sight most of the Bards that would be sent in a matter such as this.

King Leeife continued. "I believe this encounter could mark the beginning of diplomatic ties and preferred trade over raiding, contrary to the desires of some of my sea captains." Glancing at me he smiled. "This very thing is why you were brought here in the first place, Tara. It seems your presence on our shores has been noted and Kilawey seeks to open negotiations."

Alaric promptly opened the doors, calling for members of the court to join us. The council members and advisors were obviously excited to witness this historic meeting.

One, the senior member of the council spoke up. "Your Highness, what is going on, exactly? We have heard rumors of a high ranking Eirlandian ambassador arriving and requesting an immediate audience? We also heard rumors that he's a spy? How can we know? Are we all safe?

"Calm yourself, my good Jarl," replied Leeife. His papers appear authentic, and BanRigh Tara should be able to vouch for his identity in short order.

"Come, stand yourself to either side of us, you know the order and form. We must make a show of both strength and willingness to engage with the Eirlandians. They are not our enemy. Indeed I am hopeful this might mean a new relationship with them in regards to trade and even, perhaps, an exchange of ambassadors."

There was a murmur of surprise from the group, quickly silenced by a silent gesture from Alaric. The counselors took their places, and, with a nod to the guards, the doors to the Audience Chamber were again opened.

At the opening of the door, the Court Chamberlin entered, bowing, and introduced the Royal Bard from Kilawey.

Upon seeing him, I recognized him immediately. "I know him," I whispered to the King. "He is a high-ranking Bard. His name is Daman. I know him from my father's court. Being a Bard, he is known for speaking the truth."

To me, the weight of his presence suggested that the news he brought was of grave importance. My Lifenstone reacted, warming quickly against my skin.

With composed demeanors, we awaited Daman's words. Approaching the foot of the steps leading to the thrones, he respectfully bowed before addressing King Leeife in flawless Vike.

"Bard Daman, you are welcome at this court," replied Leeife in the same language. "I now ask why you have come." Daman's smile held bitterness as he acknowledged the strained relationship between Eirlandia and Vikland. He began delivering the devastating news of the tragic events that had unfolded in Kilawey.

"King Leeife, Prince Alaric, Princess Tara, members of this court," he addressed, "I bring the news of the untimely demise of Brionston, the ArdRigh of Kilawey, along with many other lesser kings of our land."

My mind grew still, all my concentration was on Daman. Being the Bard he was, he related the news without emotion, but I'm sure the incident was horrendously painful. The ArdRigh and he had been, from what I had gathered from my father, personal friends as well as Bard and ArdRigh.

"I was not present myself," Daman began, "or I would not be here to tell the tale. But a few of the guards and others who were at the back of the royal procession escaped to carry the news. This is their account." His eyes grew distant, and his voice became almost hollow, as if someone else spoke through him.

"The day was bright but cold. The ArdRigh and all his court, including several of the more important Righs, were on the last day of their annual pilgrimage to Carenow, the holy mountain sacred to the Tuatha de Danna.

Halfway up to the shrine a terrible tremor struck. Never before had the mountain shook, but it did on that day. A loud, horrific low growl seemed to emanate from the mountain, then, suddenly, the whole side of the mountain upon which the pilgrims climbed gave way. Unknown tons of rock from the cliffs above, hurtled down on the party within seconds. There was no chance of escape except for those who had not yet started the climb. There was not even time for the victims to scream, or else their cries were lost in the noise of the many rock slides.

The guards and minor officials saw the rocks start to fall and ran as quickly as possible away from the main trail and further down the mountain, leaving packs behind. The antlerres had already fled, and all were recovered later. The scattered survivors told of a great fissure that opened up low on the mountain and that it swallowed the boulders so that the town at the base was spared any destruction."

Daman paused a moment, and his eyes seemed to see us once again. "This disaster is unprecedented, Tanista Tara. Eirlandia is in turmoil, her government in disarray. It is said many of the Drui believe it to be part of an ancient prophecy foretold by the Sidheran. It cannot but be noted that no ordinary citizens were killed or even hurt.

"Tanista Tara, once of Kilbrae," Daman continued, looking directly at me, "you are destined to be our next ruler and must return to Eirlandia immediately to avert a civil war."

The weight of his words sank deep within me. The loss of my ruler and court, and the gravity of the situation, overwhelmed me. Alaric interrupted my thoughts, assuring me of his unwavering support and willingness to accompany me.

"Tara, you alone must choose," he declared. "I will stand by your side, whether you decide to go or not."

"It is as the prince says," the king added. "Because of your royal standing with both Vikland and Eirlandia, the rule of captives never returning is not enforceable. There will be no issue with you leaving here, should you decide to do so. You are a citizen of two nations, Tara, your destiny is your own to choose."

With my Lifenstone burning intensely, I knew what I had to do. Rising from my throne, I descended the steps to face Daman. Placing one hand on my heart and the other on the crown of my head, I knelt before him, a solemn gesture of commitment.

"By my heart and by my head, I pledge myself to the people and the land of Eirlandia," I recited in High Eirl, a language reserved for the most solemn occasions. The words mirrored those spoken by the ArdRigh or BanRigh during their coronation, symbolizing an unbreakable promise to the Land and the Spirits until death or formal abdication.

The significance of my pledge resonated between Daman and me, hidden from the others present. The consequences of my decision remained uncertain, but my answer had been given.

Chapter 12

The weeks that followed were filled with preparations for my return to Eirlandia. Bard Daman immediately returned home to make arrangements. Surprisingly, and to the court's consternation, Skaald Odine announced that he would be joining us on the journey. No one could dissuade him, as he believed the Spirits called him to accompany me.

"Tara will need all the support she can get," he exclaimed. "I am the equal of the ArdDrui, and he knows it. I can also act as an ambassador from this court, at least initially. Once the crisis in Eirlandia is resolved, I will inform you, King Leeife, and you can send a formal Ambassador. Who better than a Skaald to bridge the gap between our peoples and show our similarities?"

King Leeife reluctantly nodded. "Send your replacement to court as soon as possible," he commanded. "Appear before the Full Court with him to hand over your tokens of Office. Let it be clear that you will be the one to explain your departure to the entire court."

Skaald Odine simply bowed his head and left.

Several days later, Odine returned to court with a younger man at his side. The man wore attire similar to what Odine had worn when I first met him. It was announced that a new Chief Skaald would be presented, as Odine was departing with the prince and myself. The room was filled to capacity, as this would be one of our final audience days before our departure.

"My king, my prince and princess, captains, councilors, and Vikes all," Odine began, "I present to you my replacement, Skaald Freedine, as requested by King Leeife. Freedine," Odine continued, "has overseen the Skaaldara, our school for aspiring Skaalds, but he has agreed to assume this position. He has been my trusted assistant and advisor for many years."

"Do not let his appearance deceive you; he is older and wiser than he appears," Odine added, causing a murmur of surprise. "He will serve this kingdom well in the coming years, and even if I were to return, Freedine will remain the Chief Skaald."

With a ritualistic pose, Odine lifted his head and hands to the sky. "Hear my words as the words of the gods. Listen and obey him as you would obey me and the Greater Ones." Odine then divested himself of his rank, handing over his staff of office and a weighty torc, a token of his power that I had never seen him wear before.

The onlookers seemed intrigued, and some wondered about the significance of the torc. However, King Leeife appeared unfazed, suggesting that Odine had likely informed him of his actions and their reasons.

The new Chief Skaald took his place behind King Leeife's throne, while Odine stood behind Alaric. Just as they settled, the ambassador from the Formorrid, without waiting for permission, approached the throne. Though he didn't instill the same fear as Borrmid, he was still a strange-looking Formorrid. Like Borrmid, he was reptilian in looks, although not as starkly so. His face seemed a bit less fish-like, more like a frog. His eyes were dark with no pupil that I could see. I had not yet encountered the being close up, but upon seeing him I grew fearful. The Lifenstone, hidden away as it usually was under my gown, grew slightly warm, but I did not think it was feeling threatened by the creature, merely reacting to its presence. I could understand that, as something within me made me instantly dislike the ambassador and distrust him and his race. Remembering my history lessons, I recalled that the Formorrid were considered powerful mages and prone to creating chaos wherever they went in hopes of winning the advantage in any situation. I hoped that similar stories about them were known here in Vikland and that this person was not highly regarded.

Dressed in blood red instead of his usual maroon, he seemed agitated. He began speaking without ceremony, "I am bidden by my superiors to strongly protest again the prince leaving Vikland at this time. The unrest in Eirlandia is large, and we are told there are many who wish to be named to a high position in the new court. We understand that the Princess Tara must go to her people, but see no reason why Prince Alaric should accompany her at this time. His presence might create even more division and his life might be in danger as some might see him as exerting too great an influence as the Princess' husband. A better course would be to see the Princess off with a suitable guard and a few counselors and the prince could perhaps join her once the country is once again stable."

Alaric stood and addressed the emissary. "Ambassador, while we appreciate the Formorrid's concern on our behalf, I assure you I am in no greater danger than I would be on any other voyage. Contrary to what your superiors might believe, the king and I are agreed that this is a good time for explore the potential benefits of our union and to begin negotiation for trade agreements between our two nations. With Tara installed as ArdRighian, the new government will have a chance to see that we Vikes are more than raiders. Besides, we are newlywed and I have no wish to be separated from my bride for months, perhaps even years, based on some rumors and veiled threats from our long-time allies, the Formorrid."

"You have heard the Prince, Ambassador," declared Leeife. "I believe you have your answer. Tell your superiors that I fully support Prince Alaric accompanying the Tanista to her homeland, thereby showing the Vikland support without words.

You are dismissed."

As the disgruntled Formorrid left, Skaald Odine stepped between Alaric and Leeife, and gestured me close. "Be wary, you three. The Formorrid are treacherous for all they have chosen to side with the Vikes in earlier times. Their hatred for Eirlandia is well known, and I would not be surprised if they have contingency plans in place for such an event as this."

"Rest assured, Skaald," declared the king forcefully, although he kept his voice soft, "we are well aware of the enmity between the Formorria and Eirlandia. We will make sure that the trip is uneventful."

"The Drui of Eirlandia have knowledge of the Formorrid," I added. "But their information may be dated. If you could arrange, My King, to have a messenger sent to Kilawey warning them of the Formorrid threat, I would be grateful."

"It shall be done," decreed Leeife. "I shall have the Skaalds send an urgent message immediately. Skaald and Drui have worked together before, although this is not common knowledge. They have respect for each other's craft, and I am sure the message will be relayed swiftly to those who need it."

Nodding his head in dismissal, he returned to the throne and continued the interrupted audience time. Skaald Odine left immediately, and Alaric and I stayed only long enough for the most important of the petitions to be heard.

Time passed swiftly, and soon the day of our departure arrived. We set sail in three large ships, accompanied by horses, trade goods, Vike and Eirlandian servants, and chests of stolen gold to be returned to the Eirlandian people. Our arrival would replenish the royal treasury.

As we sailed, the journey proved uneventful and surprisingly swift, with perfect weather. I couldn't help but wonder if Skaald Odine's subtle gestures played a role in the favorable winds. Whether it was his doing or not, we reached Eirlandia sooner than expected.

Approaching the Dannahu River, I stood at the bow of the Wolfengaard, the same ship that had taken me away from Eirlandia.

Now it was bringing me home. As we approached the capital of my country, memories of all that had happened to me since last I had seen such a sight, many years prior, came rushing back.

I remembered standing with my father and brother on one of our ships and seeing exactly the same sight as I was now beholding. It was my first official visit to the capital. I was there to be formally introduced to the ArdRigh's court. Although still young, and not of marriageable age, I was still to be presented and the nobility present would be made aware of my father's desire to eventually see me wed. I was too young and excited to truly understand what all it meant, and I had already gotten father to promise I would be able to choose my own husband, but I still had to meet those young men and even boys who might one day ask my hand in binding.

I remembered also meeting the ArdRigh and Royal Consort, and how kind the consort was, taking me off after formal presentation to a small garden where she asked about my life at my father's court, and did I remember my mother at all.

I know I had felt a little strange and awkward during that meeting, and sorry I couldn't tell her about my mother, but realizing now that the woman was my aunt, her questions seemed much more normal for someone trying to get information about a sibling they had lost contact with.

Slowly the feelings of regret, of longing for the past, and even remembered joy faded. In its place rose feelings of pride and determination. I was not a young, foolish princess, I was Tanista and soon to be ArdRighian of this land and its people. I had to look forward, not behind.

Kilawey, situated inland and protected from Vike raids, appeared before me. Its white walls rose on a hill overlooking the wharves, said to be created by the power of the Sidheran after a battle with the Formorrid.

Notably absent were the flags of the ArdRigh, replaced instead by dark purple banners signifying mourning and royal death. It confirmed the truth of Bard Daman's words, filling me with both hope and the weight of responsibility.

Upon docking, I noticed royal guards and Bard Daman waiting for us, along with several saddled horses. The guards seemed more than necessary, and I observed that some of the horses' gear was of finer quality.

Alaric, Sven, Odine, Vilk, and I were on deck together. Alaric reassured me that he would observe and learn, deferring to my authority as ruler of Kilawey. We disembarked, mounted the steeds, and were swiftly escorted to the Nementon by Bard Daman, who seemed concerned for our safety.

Inside the Greater Hall, the council members who could attend greeted us. It was decided to convene a Greater Council at the next new moon, seven days hence. Alaric remained quiet, while Odine, Sven, and I participated in the discussions.

Later, as we sat together in our chambers, Alaric looked around and shook his head. Turning to me, he said, "I never believed the stories of your land and its riches. Tales of how grand everyone lived, even commoners, seemed like fairy tales." But I have observed your buildings, your citizens as we came to the palace, the state of your streets, even your ability to have water and bathing facilities so close and convenient with hot water at a touch, and I have come to realize the stories, at least some of them, are true.

How is it you people are so much more advanced in the sciences, in building, in many things, it seems, than we?"

I smiled and took his hand. "Oh, my dear one, we are older than you know. And we have the advantage of a long and prosperous relationship with our underground neighbors, the Sidheran. They have imparted to us much of their knowledge and skills. We also share with them an ability that seems, for the most part, lacking in your people."

Alaric looked at me quizzically. "What ability?" he queried. "I have heard the name and know they live underground, having little to do with the Eirlandians, at least presently, although I guess there are old folktales of them once being much more involved with your race.

At this revelation, I admit to chuckling. It had never occurred to me that the Sidheran were relatively unknown to the Vike.

"Oh, Alaric, our history with the Sidheran is long and will take some time fully explain. They are magic workers, as are many of our people, especially our Drui, our Skaalds, if you will," I added at his look of confusion. "There is much about us you do not know, but you will have time to learn all about us. We have Bards, teachers, who will be happy to instruct you on Eirlandian laws, lore, practices, etc. This time it will be you who will be the student, not I. I can also help, but much of my time will be spent catching up with all I need to know to rule here properly and there will be little free time for either of us."

"Then I think we should take advantage of this free time while we have it," purred Alaric in my ear. "Come, wife, let us see just how comfortable the beds are here." Laughing, I led him into the inner chamber and closed the door.

Chapter 13

My first few weeks in Eirlandia don't require much detail. The events during that time have been extensively documented in my papers of state, council meetings, and declarations. I owe my profound gratitude to Bard Daman, ArdDrui Loockan, and ArdSkaald Odine for their constant guidance and support in matters that were entirely new to me.

Alaric sat beside me during the discussions but refrained from actively participating or expressing his opinions. His silence and patience seemed to win the favor of many, as his behavior was contrary to what my courtiers had anticipated.

After more than a month, the leaders of all the clans of Eirlandia convened at Kilawey. The process of confirming my claim as the next ruler of Eirlandia could finally begin.

The confirmation ceremony was scheduled to take place during the Harvest Moon, which was only a week away. The announcement had been widely circulated, and the Righs of all the tribes, along with their Tanists, had arrived. Most of them appeared inclined to recognize my title as the ArdRighian, a ruling position that had not been held before, although some tribes had previously been governed by female rulers.

While the Lesser Righs recognized the leadership qualities in Alaric, whom they respected for his strength and adherence to our ways, there was also appreciation for ArdSkaald Odine's diplomatic skills. The friendship between ArdSkaald Odine and ArdDrui Loockan worked in my favor as well.

As the day drew to a close, Bard Daman entered the Audience Chamber, making a bold entrance while carrying the Silver Bough, a branch of bells used to signify important announcements. A sense of unease gripped me upon seeing this, as I sensed that it could only bring unsettling news.

"Tanista Tara, Consort Alaric, esteemed members of this court, and all present, lend me your ears," Bard Daman proclaimed, approaching the dais. He respectfully bowed before Alaric and me, then turned to face the gathering of courtiers, warriors, and citizens. With three ringing tolls of the bells, customary for significant proclamations, he began speaking.

"Listen now to the words of the Seers, the Lookouts, and the counsel of the Drui Court, for we bring you grievous tidings and profound sorrow. ArdDrui Loockan is no more. He was brutally murdered during a ritual, the assailant remaining unknown but suspected to be a Formorrid. Loockan did not meet his end by arrow, sword, or knife, but rather by dark magic. Witnesses among the Drui reported a sinister cloud descending from the sky, enveloping Loockan within the Holy Circle. He had no chance to cry out before his lifeless body fell to the ground, and the cloud dissipated like smoke. The healers present confirmed that Loockan was already deceased when he hit the ground, his heart ceased, and his spirit departed his body."

A stunned silence fell upon the court as I, along with everyone present, absorbed this horrendous news. Eventually, I found my voice and inquired, "What guidance does the Drui Court offer in light of this tragedy? Is there any further information we have regarding this incident?"

"Our most skilled Seers managed to trace the source of the dark cloud to a small island off our coast. Scouts were dispatched and reported signs of campfires and shelters. From the remnants left behind, it was deduced that the occupants were Formorrid, likely priests or magicians of their kind."

"The Council deemed it crucial to relay this information with utmost urgency. They believe that the confirmation of your ascension must proceed swiftly, granting you and your Consort the authority to lead our nation in this time of crisis. The Drui Council possesses knowledge concerning you that will be revealed during the Confirmation. Your unique abilities, coupled with the support of the Vikes, who shall stand as our allies, are seen as pivotal in confronting this threat."

At this, ArdSkaald Odine raised his staff and spoke as both a High Skaald of the Vikes and their representative. "My fellow Eirlandians, I pledge the support of the Vikes in any battle you may face, including those against the Formorrid. I offer my expertise in the Other Realm alongside my Drui brethren for this undertaking."

Pandemonium erupted among the crowd, with everyone speaking or shouting at once. Many expressed a desire to hunt down and punish the Formorrid immediately.

I managed to calm the hot-headed individuals, reminding them that the actions of a small, potentially independent group did not condemn an entire race. While I acknowledged the need to identify any Formorrid among us, I emphasized the importance of treating them with respect. I suggested that we invite them to consult on matters related to the relationship between our peoples under the pretense of the Tanista seeking their counsel.

Several warriors and others promptly left the hall. The warriors likely set off to rally their people, while the others spread the news. If any Formorrid spies lurked among us, they would have overheard my proclamation and intentions.

"Esteemed Righs and members of the High Court, I propose that we adjourn to private chambers to discuss this matter more extensively," I announced. Rising from my seat, I signaled for Bard Daman to lead the way. With Alaric at my side and my counselors and righs following, we exited the audience hall and entered an adjoining chamber where we could deliberate in private.

Once inside, I dispatched attendants to bring refreshments and candles to ensure adequate lighting as evening approached. We were unsure how long our seclusion would last, but darkness was imminent.

I also requested a map of Eirlandia and any available information regarding the whereabouts of the Formorrid. Alaric informed me that the Dun we had previously visited was only a few hours' travel from Eirlandian territory, yet its location remained hidden through Formorrid magic, rendering it absent from our maps. However, he believed he could provide an approximate location on a map, and if necessary, he could reach out to his father to arrange for Vike troops to attack the Dun. Unless the Formorrid had spies who overheard Odine's proclamation, they would likely permit the Vikes to land.

As we briefly paused the discussions and preparations, the Righs approached me in a group, followed by Bard Daman.

"Tanista," one of the elder Righs spoke up, "we would appreciate it if Bard Daman could shed light on the 'special abilities' he mentioned earlier. Additionally, we are curious to know the circumstances surrounding your selection as Tanista, if you are willing to share."

I turned to Bard Daman, who wore a smile that conveyed both encouragement and a hint of secrecy, reminiscent of a cat that knew the whereabouts of a hidden mouse.

Turning my attention back to the Righs, I addressed them, saying, "Gentles, I am as eager as you to know. I was never fully informed about why the late ArdRigh chose me as Tanista, nor am I aware of any special gifts or abilities I may possess, as I do not lay claim to any."

I directed my gaze toward Bard Daman, who still wore a faint smile. "Bard Daman," I spoke formally, "if it pleases you, please enlighten us. If I am to be confirmed, as the Drui Council advises, it is imperative that we all understand why."

Bard Daman nodded, and we took our seats. Then he turned to me and said, "Tanista, you must reveal the Lifenstone, which you have wisely kept concealed for these past months. It will serve as proof for what I am about to disclose."

Suppressing my surprise and consternation at his knowledge of my secret, I retrieved the Lifenstone from its hiding place on the chain around my neck. The stone felt warm to the touch, and its radiance appeared more vibrant than ever. Only I seemed to notice a faint humming sound emanating from it. As the stone came into view, several of the older Righs instinctively made the Sign of the Fae, displaying either fear or wonder—I couldn't discern which.

"This stone," I began, addressing everyone present, "belonged to my mother. Through it, I have glimpsed her and received teachings that I cannot recall, no matter how hard I try. I don't know if Bard Daman possesses the means to unlock my mother's knowledge, but I hope so, as the 'gifts' I may possess remain dormant."

Bard Daman lowered his head respectfully. "I do not possess the knowledge myself, but the new ArdDrui does, and he shall join us within a day or two at most. However, I do possess knowledge of your bloodline and the reason behind your ability to carry and utilize a Lifenstone."

Looking around at those present, Bard Daman appeared to note the different reactions in those gathered.

"Some among you are already familiar with this gem, as I could tell from your reactions," he continued. "Others are unaware, as they were never taught about it. While some consider Lifenstones mere legends, it is evident that at least one has survived the Last Great War, and I believe there are more waiting to be discovered."

A murmur went through the crowd, although individual comments were not discernable. It was obvious, however, that this statement was meant with surprise and disbelief from many.

"Tanista Tara received this stone from her mother, as she mentioned." Bard Daman continued, pretending not to hear the murmurings. "However, what she didn't know, until now, is that her mother was a

Sidheran. Furthermore, her mother, Neeve, belonged to the royal line of the Sidheran and was the sister of our late ArdRigh's life mate."

There were whisperings at Daman's words, and Alaric and I looked at each other. We both knew that I had learned of my mother's identity already, but I shook my head slightly to indicate that I was not going to share that information at this time.

"What the court is yet to learn," Daman continued seamlessly, "is that the High Consort Mayveer is alive and well. She voluntarily withdrew from court life and returned to the Sidheran when it became clear that her relationship with ArdRigh Brionston would not yield any heirs.

"But she knew that her sister had a daughter, and she arranged for a Lifenstone to be bestowed upon her niece as a memento of her mother and a safeguard against harm."

The Bard reached his hand toward me, and indicated he would like to hold the Lifenstone. I nodded slightly, then took the gem from around my neck and presented it to him. Careful to hold the gem by its chain, Daman held it high so that most could see it.

"This particular Lifenstone carries a hidden message and a spell for unlocking the knowledge that Tara now possesses. The activation occurred during her voyage to Vikland. The spell was designed to remain dormant until the time was right, which is now. The ArdDrui has obtained the means to unleash the Sidheran knowledge and the power that Tara now holds."

As Daman spoke I recalled some of what I had learned on that voyage. I knew my heritage, and the thought that Sidheran blood flowed in my veins brought mixed feelings. The Sidherans were a powerful mage race. They were very old, much older than we Eirlandians, and had always been here, whereas we had arrived from a distant land, refugees from a terrible earthquake that had destroyed our old island home. The Sidherans had once lived above ground, but had yielded the land above to us after a battle in which our famous Bard, Ammerigan, had defeated their most powerful mage, Bonne. In order to keep the land from being destroyed, the Sidherans withdrew from the surface and built a strange and wondrous country beneath our feet. To this day there were some places that we Eirlandians were forbidden to disturb, as they were close to entrances to the Sidheran realm.

Coming back to the moment, I listened to Daman's words, which both frightened and intrigued me. What had the Lifenstone taught me that I couldn't remember? My Aunt Mayveer was alive? Would I have the opportunity to meet her, to learn from her? How had this secret been kept hidden for so long? These thoughts raced through my mind, though I maintained a composed expression. Glancing at Alaric, I saw him pale and tight-lipped. He knew certain aspects, particularly about my mother, but the rest was new to him. I wondered if he felt anger toward me for withholding this secret.

ArdSkaald Odine was the first to break the silence. "Bard Daman, we have all heard revelations that were previously unknown to us. Some among us are hearing these details for the first time, while others are only now filling in missing pieces. I ask you; do you know the name of the new ArdDrui, or shall that remain undisclosed until their arrival? Furthermore, is there any additional information you possess regarding the Formorrid threat?"

Chief Bard Daman respectfully inclined his head toward Odine before responding. "As for the new ArdDrui's name, it is Labraird. He is a skilled healer and practitioner of magic. He is among the few Drui capable of reading and harnessing the power of a Lifenstone, thanks to his Sidheran lineage."

That revelation took me by surprise. The Sidherans were a recluse race, and I had always felt these underground dwellers considered themselves superior to us surface dwellers. It is true they were here before us, but our legends say we had defeated them in battle and that was when they yielded us the surface. 'Perhaps,' I thought, 'our legends aren't altogether truthful.'

Looking around the room, Daman continued, "I am unaware of any further intelligence concerning the threat beyond what I revealed in the open court. It is likely that ArdDrui Labraird will possess additional knowledge upon his arrival."

"For now, our primary focus must be the safety of Tanista Tara. Additionally, it is essential to confirm her as the ArdRighian with Prince Alaric as her Royal Consort and Battle Lord as soon as possible. We need not proceed with the coronation rites, only the confirmation along with the proclamation disseminated to all the tribes. This will grant Tara and Alaric the lawful authority to convene the tribes and address this threat."

"I understand that you all have your own tribal realms to protect, but Tara and Alaric carry the responsibility for the entire nation, not just specific territories. You are familiar with our late ArdRigh's intentions to bring Tara here and have her confirmed as Tanista before her capture. You agreed with his reasoning, or else Lady Tara would not have been confirmed. However, she has been, so that is no longer a matter of debate. There is no better leader in this critical time, no one possessing the necessary power, resolve, and knowledge to combat this threat. Where Tara's battle leadership may fall short, her consort, Prince Alaric, shall fill the gap. I assure you that the Great Ones have orchestrated their presence in our time of need. Let us set aside petty aspirations and unite, for if we fail to do so, Eirlandia will surely succumb to the Formorrid menace, and all that we have achieved shall be in vain."

The Righs, averting their gazes, exhibited a range of reactions; some sheepish, others tinged with rebellion, and a few on the brink of despair or perhaps hope. None met Daman's or my eyes for a brief moment.

After a moment of silence, the hall erupted in a babble of conflicting voices. The younger Righs appeared to be fine with me becoming ArdRighian, but most of the older ones seemed to have an issue with several things about me, including my sex, age and lack of experience. The fact that I came towing a Vike prince as my consort was also a matter of hot debate.

I felt grateful, then, for the law that forbids weapons of any kind within the royal audience chambers. The most that could happen would be a fist fight or two, and those would be put down swiftly by the Fighdrui guards, who already stood on alert.

Alaric touched my arm, and he looked a bit nonplussed at the reaction of the Righs. Perhaps he thought they would accept me without discussion. Obviously he did not understand us very well.

Just as I was about to signal Bard Daman to exercise some control over the debate, something unexpected occurred. Righ Anluon, the eldest of the provincial righs and ruler of the Tribe of Loughnass, rose to his feet. He had been sitting with several other of the older righs, they had been discussing something, but in the din it had been impossible to know exactly what was being said. Righ Anluon was well respected and at his action, all the other righs became quiet and reseated themselves.

The old righ looked to his right and left and then centered his gaze on me. "On this day, I pledge my life, honor, and the welfare of my tribe to our new ArdRighian, Tara of Eirlandia and Sidhera, and her consort, Prince Alaric of Vikland," he solemnly declared in High Eire, the language of solemn vows. Drawing his sword, he placed it at my feet.

In accordance with tradition, I accepted his sword and raised it high, then reversed it and drove the point downward, touching the floor before me. Gently placing my hand on the keen edge, I pressed just enough to draw a drop of blood. Returning the sword to Righ Anluon, I spoke in High Eire once more, "Your sword is consecrated with my blood, just as your land and people are consecrated to me. I accept your loyalty and vow to govern you to the best of my abilities for as long as the people and gods desire."

One by one, the other Righs pledged their swords and the lives of their tribes to me. With each oath, I repeated the phrase that came to me in the moment, despite its unfamiliarity until then.

Casting a quick glance at Bard Daman, I noticed a mix of astonishment, surprise, and respect in his eyes. I suspected that he understood I hadn't known the words beforehand, that they had been bestowed upon me by the Lifenstone.

After the official confirmation concluded, we left the Council Chambers, bypassing the Audience Room. Bard Daman made an announcement that, due to the grave news, court proceedings would adjourn for the day. However, he promised that a "momentous announcement" would be made at the next Nooning of the sun.

Alaric and I retired to our quarters, where we held an extensive discussion with our entourage. We instructed them to remain vigilant and prohibit any strangers from entering, regardless of their official appearance. Vilk was assigned the task of vetting unknown individuals seeking entry to our chambers.

Once Vilk departed, Alaric slumped wearily in his seat and motioned for me to join him. "So it begins, my love," he whispered. "You mustn't be afraid or troubled by withholding knowledge of the Lifenstone's power from me. I was aware of your Sidheran heritage and suspected that you possessed unique abilities or marks. Skaald Odine later confirmed this to me after we arrived in Vikland."

"I don't comprehend any of this," I replied, still grappling with the revelations. "What have we done to provoke the Formorrid? Why would they murder our ArdDrui? It makes no sense to me. For generations, we have coexisted separately, avoiding one another's paths. What has changed?"

"I do not possess the answers, my eaglet," he responded. "However, I suspect that you are the catalyst for this change. For some reason, the Formorrid fear you. That became evident even at the Dun. They fear you even more now, as you are on the verge of becoming the

ArdRighian, and they are displeased by my presence. I believe this combination is what troubles them. We, who should be enemies, are instead husband and wife, uniting the Vike and Eirlandian peoples. If we were to stand together, our nations would be a formidable force against any adversary. Perhaps the Formorrid fear that we will ally against them."

"By attacking and slaying the ArdDrui, they have compelled our response. With you here at the time, they must surely realize that we can call upon the Vike for assistance in this battle, should the need arise," I added.

"This doesn't feel right." Alaric declared. "It appears to be a ploy, but for what purpose, I cannot fathom. I suspect the Formorrid believed that the Vike would side with them rather than with your people, but I am uncertain why."

"Perhaps," I interrupted, "they hoped this event would demoralize us and plunge us into panic or despair. If so, they do not understand our resilience. No leadership vacancy remains unfilled for long, especially when the predecessor is slain. We must await their next move."

Standing up, I walked over to the window. My restlessness made it impossible to remain still. "You are correct; an envoy must be dispatched to the Sidheran. I will raise this matter with the council later. I believe Bard Daman would be the most suitable candidate for the mission."

Alaric spoke up. "Why is that? Is the Bard someone special to you?"

Looking at him, I was surprised to see what appeared to be jealousy sparking in his eyes. "Oh, Alaric, do not be jealous of Daman. He is no threat. I suggest him because I happen to know he is related, distantly, to a member of the Sidheran High Council, a second or third cousin I believe. The point being he spent some time in Sidhera in his youth and the Sidherans know him well, and trust him.

I only hope that the Sidheran will aid us. I have much to learn about my mother's people. As I have mentioned, I think, these are a reclusive people, who existed here long before Eirlandians ever came to these shores. There is much about themselves they keep secret. I really only know that they are known, feared, and respected for their mage abilities."

"Come here, my love," Alaric beckoned softly. "Come and rest for a moment. I fear that our separation is imminent, for if there is actual warfare, I must assume the role of Battle Leader. Let us seize this time for ourselves and momentarily set aside the troubles of the world."

Nodding, I joined him once more, and for a while, the world around us faded away.

Chapter 14

In just a few days, the new ArdDrui arrived in Kilawey. Labraird bore no resemblance to his predecessor, as he exuded vitality, strength, and power. His intense green eyes seemed capable of penetrating my every thought, should he choose to do so.

We convened in a small chamber deep within the Nementon. The ArdDrui had requested my presence, along with ArdSkaald Odine and Bard Daman, but no one else. In his request, he emphasized the importance of magical power and ability, deeming it unsafe for others to join us at this time. The formidable power of the Lifenstone and the spell to unlock its potential necessitated a limited audience, thus I found myself in that chamber with my two magical advisors.

The room bore evidence of its use for spellcasting and magic, with intricate invocations to the gods etched on every wall and above the door. Though devoid of windows, symbols adorned the air vents, allowing fresh air and the escape of herbal smoke and incense. The floor displayed a mysterious design surrounding the central carving of the Interwoven Ring of Eternity.

A palpable power emanated from that spot, while the Lifenstone on my breast blazed with life and warmth, carefully shielded from direct contact with my skin.

ArdDrui Labraird ignited a small incense burner and traversed the room, chanting in an unfamiliar language. Though I couldn't comprehend the words, I sensed a cleansing and blessing taking place.

He motioned for Daman and Odine to guide me into the circle of power. They stood outside the intricate carving, holding my hands as I extended my arms. I wondered at their positioning and would soon discover the reason.

Approaching with a staff in hand, the ArdDrui possessed a large crystal atop it—a Lifenstone, much like the one I had encountered before. Two of these crystals together were a rarity, and I silently hoped Labraird was aware of the potential power and took precautions. He extended his staff, bringing the stone within inches of mine, and recited unintelligible words. Light erupted from his crystal, striking mine, and in the brilliance, I closed my eyes and saw my mother standing before me.

Having never seen my mother in life, and seeing her only vaguely in my dreams and visions about the ship taking me to Vikland, I looked at her closely, hoping to see something of myself in her.

She was tall, as tall as my father had been. Her hair was bound up in a veil of white, and I could not see the color. Her face was delicate and pale, with slightly slanted eyes the color the ocean at noon, dark blue and grey. She was, by all standards of beauty, the most beautiful woman I had ever seen either in person or in paintings.

One thing was certain, I had gotten my hair and eyes from my father, not my mother. I was, I admit, a bit disappointed in that fact, although I knew I was thought of as beautiful, I felt my mother surpassed me in the regard in every way.

She had the look of the goddess Brigitta about her, although she was obviously mortal. She was definitely of Sidheran blood, not Eirlandian. I had only seen one or two Sidherans since my return to Eirlandia, but all bore the same coloration and slightly slanted eyes.

My mother could not actually be presented, a logical part of my mind insisted. This was some magical projection. Still, the image evoked the same emotions of both longing and loss, hope and fear as would have been present if this truly was my mother.

The image looked at me directly then, and a smile lit up her features, suddenly making her seem much more real and human. "Greetings, my daughter," she said gently. "It gladdens my heart to see you grown so comely, as well as strong in character and will. You will need your moral strength and your strong will in these times." Then her face became more remote and she looked a bit above me.

"The time has come," she announced. "The ArdDrui will unlock the power of the Lifenstone. You will experience some discomfort, daughter, followed by darkness. When you awaken, you shall possess full knowledge and control over the Lifenstone—this one and all others. It is necessary to ensure that no Lifenstone falls into the hands of the Formorrid and is used against us."

She drew closer, her hand enclosing the stone on my breast, unaffected by the searing heat. "Prepare yourself, Daughter," she whispered.

Then, my mind erupted. I felt as if I could taste the colors within the room. Looking around for a moment I realized that the blues tasted of berries, the reds and pinks of fresh meat, the yellows smelled like daisies. Every sound was amplified and imbued with emotions. I could literally taste the feeling of fear that I myself was feeling; it was like tasting rust in water from an old pipe. Drawing a breath filled my nose and mouth with a multitude of tastes and scents. Looking around I felt as if I could see every detail of everyone's clothing, hair, skin, everything, until the overwhelming power drove me into unconsciousness.

When I regained consciousness, I found myself in a small yet comfortable bed, evidently in a different room. The Lifenstone had cooled, but a newfound spark pulsed within its core.

A discreet cough alerted me to ArdDrui Labraird's presence, holding a steaming cup of aromatic liquid. "Drink, Tanista. These herbs will clear your head and restore your strength," he instructed.

I complied, feeling better before the cup was emptied.

Though I cannot recall all that was said, Labraird provided me with extensive instructions on the use and potential of the Master Lifenstone. Time passed as meals arrived, and I rested intermittently.

While I now possessed the knowledge to unleash the stone's power, I also needed to understand its limitations and the situations warranting its unrestricted employment.

As I have mentioned in my writings before, I dare not go into details regarding this knowledge for fear of the Lifenstone being used against our people at some point in the future should it fall into the wrong hands.

Moreover, I delved into the history and lore of my mother's people, discovering my role as a Child of Prophecy. The Sidheran would go to great lengths to ensure the realization of these prophecies-the Prophecy of Doom, as the Formorrid called it, and the Prophecy of Redemption, as the Sidherans named it.

Finally, Labraird deemed me ready, and I was escorted to a small chamber just outside the council room, where I bathed and donned the formal robes of state.

Adorned with the Cloak of Authority and wielding the Staff of Power, I emerged through the door, no longer the Tanista but now the ArdRighian of Eirlandia. Representatives from every clan, trade, and Drui branch crowded the hall to pay their respects and pledge their oaths of fealty to the new ArdRighian.

For the first time, I beheld and sat upon the High Throne, absent in the Royal Hall during the interregnum periods. Typically, a Regent governed when the Tanista was not of age. As with the Righs in the Council Chambers, the heads of the Greater Families, various Guilds, and Armed Forces stepped forward to offer their oaths of fealty, receiving mine in return. The Drui Class had already pledged through the former ArdDrui, yet Labraird personally approached to swear his allegiance. Representatives from different disciplines of Fighdrui— teachers, bards, healers, seers, scholars—likewise presented themselves.

The ceremony was long and somewhat tedious, but I felt no weariness, as if the Lifenstone continued to invigorate and sustain me. Finally, the oaths were exchanged, and the last of the Drui bestowed their blessings upon my reign and the land. We adjourned to the banquet hall for a meal, where I learned that the Formorrid had been traced to an island just beyond our borders. Presently, we could do nothing to apprehend the murderers, as they had temporarily eluded capture. However, King Leeife had dispatched Vike warships, which would reach the island in a matter of days.

Chapter 15

Within a few days of the crowning, we received word that the Vike warships had arrived at the Formorrid's home island and surrounded it, laying siege to those inside.

However, the Formorrid wielded weapons and power. They bombarded the ships with large lead spheres, damaging a few of them. Though no magical devices had been employed yet, the Vikes were certain it was only a matter of time.

We also received word of a group of Formorrid mages holed up in a cave near the western coast of Eirlandia. The area around the cave was brimming with magical wards, making it impossible for scouts to approach. However, our Far Seers reported signs of a military buildup in the area, concealed by magic. In response, Alaric took command of our forces, exercising his right and duty as Battle Leader. He dispatched scouts accompanied by Drui skilled in Far Seeing and protective magic.

Subsequently, he organized the nation's forces, summoning the nearest Righs to gather their troops at a rendezvous point near the magical border of the Formorrid's camp. He then instructed all other tribes to prepare their troops and await his summons. He aimed to establish a robust defense line, forcing the Formorrid to confront our entire land and all our forces before reaching Kilawey.

"If we can't stop them," he confided one evening, "we can at least delay and weaken them. Hopefully, by the time they reach here, the royal forces will be able to finish them off."

Within half a moon of my crowning, my Battle Leader consort led a substantial contingent of soldiers and Drui. The Nemed grew quieter in their absence, as many from the Royal Fighdrui contingent joined Alaric.

ArdDrui Labraird remained in Kilawey, accompanied by ArdSkaald Odine and several other seasoned and powerful Drui magic workers. For several days, I learned and studied under Labraird and Odine. I discovered that, with the help of the Lifenstone, I could wield both Vike and Eirlandian magic.

One such example is when the ArdDrui set me a task to create a protective barrier around me capable of withstanding attacks from both himself and ArdSkaald Odine.

We were in a small courtyard used by the Drui for just such magical practice. As such it was fully shielded so that whatever magic was unleashed it would do no harm to the building itself or even to the wielders of the spells.

I stood facing the two men, the Lifenstone now encased in a protective wire cage so it no longer rested directly on my skin.

"The magic is too powerful for direct contact with your skin," Labraird had told me. "The wire cage will direct all the energy outward, otherwise you could be severely burned, even killed by the energy released."

I cupped my hands to either side of the wire, and silently recited the incantation I had been taught to call up the barrier. The Lifenstone responded and I could literally see the energy pouring from the stone to create an enclosure around me. I remember I smiled grimly; confident I had mastered this skill.

Labraird was first, his attacks creating sparks against the barriers as they connected. But none were able to penetrate. Then came Odine, but his was a surprise.

"You do well against Eirlandian magic," he remarked. "But what about Formorrid? I have learned some of their skills, since the Vike were once staunch and long allies with them. Their magic is quite different and very strong. I think you will need more than this barrier to withstand what I now send. Prepare, Tara, this could be unpleasant."

Then he pointed his staff at me, and a stream of what appeared to be fire came from its large black stone that decorated its terminus. I had assumed the stone only for decoration, but I was wrong. The moment the flame hit the barrier, I knew it wouldn't hold for long. I remember panicking a bit, until I heard my mother's voice.

"Tell the Lifenstone to use the 'Danu Defense.' It will know and react. Command it now and remember to do so in High Eirlandian, which is also Sidheran."

The words were out before my mother's voice finished echoing in my mind. At those two words the barrier flashed a bright blue, and the stream of fire was extinguished faster than one could snap their fingers.

Odine's face registered both surprise and admiration for a brief moment. "Ha!" Cried Labraird victoriously! "I told you, Odine, that she knew more than she realized! That was Sidheran magery, not Eirlandian!"

Indeed, from that point on I found that spells of the Sidheran would immediately come to mind when the situation so required, even though I received no formal training in Sidheran magic.

Also during this time, we sent a request for aid to the Sidheran and awaited their response before I embarked to face the Formorrid. According to Labraird, my presence was crucial for victory. He repeatedly referred to me as the Chosen One, explaining that my Lifenstone was the most potent ever produced by the Sidheran.

This conversation occurred the evening of the incident with the Lifenstone against Odine's surprise Formorrid magic attack. We were sitting in the outdoor dining area of the Drui quarters, relaxing after the evening meal, when Labraird suddenly looked up from his cup of mead and regarded me intensely.

"My ArdRighian," he began very formally, "I think it time you learned a few things about your Lifenstone and even yourself. There are a few things I do not believe your mother has told you."

I straightened up, and put down my cup. "What is it? What haven't I been told?"

"You are, I firmly believe, the designated One of the Prophecy of the Awen. That prophecy states that at a time of great tragedy for Eirlandia, a child would be born who was both Eirlandian and Sidheran, and that this child would inherit the legendary powers of the Great Mages of Old who first forged the alliance between Eirlandia and Sidhera.

This One would be 'unnoticed in youth, but whose forced journey to an enemy land would signal the beginning of a new era for both nations'".

Labraird took a small sip of his mead then continued. "Your Lifenstone is, I believe, the First One, the one that was meant to be the master over all the others who would come after it. Your mother wore this Lifenstone both as a symbol of her station within Sidhera and as a protection for the Lifenstone against it being stolen by rivals. It was created to serve as the Master Lifenstone over all others. It grants you command over the elements, within reasonable limits. It has now linked to you, preventing others from using it."

Labraird took another drink, this time of water from the glass on the table. "The fact it has bonded with you offers protection against the Formorrid. But also means that no one else can employ it in your absence or after your demise, at least not in time to make a difference during a battle."

I looked at Labraird with a questioning gaze, and he further elaborated. "Re-keying the stone is possible, but it requires time and a Master Mage of the Sidheran. It's highly unlikely that one of their Masters will be present on the battlefield, even if some of the lesser mages and soldiers are."

I absorbed his words later as I practiced spells and honed my ability to wield the power bestowed by the Lifenstone. Around a tenight after Alaric's departure, we received news that the Sidheran had agreed to assist us. It was none other than Principia Mayveer herself who brought the news, along with her own counsel.

Amidst the ongoing preparations for battle, I continued to hold court, ensuring the kingdom was governed. I established a Royal Council to rule in my absence, but there were numerous matters requiring my attention until then. After settling a dispute between two rival tribes over the interpretation of the law, the chamber doors suddenly became veiled in a thick, glowing mist, reminiscent of the radiance emitted by my Lifenstone during use. The guards attempted to enter the mist but found themselves immobilized.

"Ah, the Sidheran," remarked Labraird dryly. "They seldom bother with doors these days." As he spoke, the mist dissipated, revealing a tall, light-skinned woman with white hair, exuding ethereal beauty, standing just inside the chamber.

An audible gasp escaped those in attendance as they recognized her. "Principia Mayveer," Daman breathed in disbelief and awe.

The woman surveyed the room, exchanging smiles with a few courtiers, then gracefully approached, almost gliding, until she stood before the throne. She bowed as one ArdRighian to another, displaying neither deference nor arrogance but a respectful confidence.

"ArdRighian Tara of Eirlandia," she began in a mellifluous voice, resonating with evident authority. "I bring you greetings from your kin and allies, the Sidheran. The High Council has observed the resurgence of the Ancient Enemy, and we stand ready to aid you in defending Eirlandia, a land as much ours as it is yours. The Sidheran Mages are gathering as we speak, and all the Lifenstones are attuned to yours. As your blood relative, I shall act as the temporary liaison between you and the Sidheran forces, as I am more adept at long- distance thought communication than you are." Her final sentence was spoken softly, intended only for my ears and those of my closest advisors.

Her words hinted at knowledge I had yet to acquire, as no one had taught me the art of transmitting thoughts. A glance at Labraird confirmed his lack of awareness, leaving me to wonder whether it was an inherent ability of the Sidheran or the Lifenstone.

"Welcome, Principia Mayveer," I responded formally, projecting my voice to ensure it carried. "I am honored to meet my mother's sister. Your aid is wholeheartedly welcomed, as is that of your compatriots. I am certain you can impart much wisdom, for I am still unfamiliar with magic and must learn swiftly."

"I am honored, ArdRighian, and I stand ready to assist, as do all the Sidheran," she replied with formality.

I rose, compelled by an internal urging I couldn't fully comprehend. "Come, Aunt Mayveer, let us retire. The audience has concluded for the day anyway, a fact you undoubtedly anticipated when timing your arrival. We have much to discuss and little time in which to do so."

I descended from the throne, and Mayveer, accompanied by Odine, Daman, Labraird, and my ever-present guard Vilk, walked with me through the now-silent hall and into the smaller council chamber beyond.

Once inside, I sent Vilk to fetch refreshments. We gathered around the round table at the chamber's center. To my surprise, Mayveer conjured a map of Eirlandia and the surrounding islands seemingly out of thin air.

Raising an eyebrow but refraining from comment, I witnessed the manifestation. Stories of the Sidheran's abilities to move objects and even individuals from place to place had circulated, rendering it an unremarkable feat among them. Mayveer spread the map before us, indicating the precise locations of the Formorrid. She also pointed out a golden circle near one of the large Formorrid encampments, an emblem absent from any other maps or charts.

"This circle marks an entrance to Sidhera," she explained. "The Formorrid are unaware of its existence, but if they were to discover it, they could potentially breach the entrance and gain access to our realm. Such an outcome must be prevented at all costs, both for the Sidheran and the Eirlandians. We, the Sidheran, are relatively few in number, and the loss of a single life would be devastating. Moreover, the knowledge and weapons the Formorrid would acquire are beyond the scope of warning."

Her voice turned cold and demanding. "ArdRighian, this is where you must make your stand. You must defeat the Formorrid encamped so close to our entrance. They are the ones who killed your former ArdDrui, and they possess advanced magical skills and knowledge."

"We are certain the Formorrid suspect the existence of a Sidhera entrance near their camp, which is why they chose this location. Otherwise, there would be no strategic value to the area," she continued.

I glanced at the others present, and they all nodded in agreement. "The protection of the Sidheran Tuath is paramount," Labraird declared. "Too much is at stake. The fate of Sidhera is entwined with the fate of Eirlandia, as our earliest Drui, Ammerigan, was told when the Sons of Eirl first arrived and negotiated settlement rights with the Sidheran. Our destinies are intertwined."

"Even among my people," added ArdSkaald Odine, "tales of the history of Sidhera and Eirlandia have always recounted the mystical bond between your two clans. Many Skaalds believe that all three clans are actually related, with ancient roots. Perhaps now, when Vike, Eirlandian, and Sidheran are uniting in a common cause, the prophecies may be in play. There are vague writings in our scrolls that speak of this time, when such an alliance would rise to fight a single enemy. Some of my brethren dismiss these writings, but now I understand that this battle is indeed the one foretold."

"Then let it be so," I replied quietly. "Prepare all that is necessary. We depart at the rising of the Reborn Moon."

At that moment, Vilk returned with a group of servants carrying water, mead, ale, cakes, and fruit.

Vilk took one look at me and declared, "If you leave without me, Alaric will surely behead me when he discovers. I have no desire to be headless. I am coming with you."

"Of course you are," I responded with a near-laugh, for the expression on his face was so comical that it lightened the atmosphere. He grinned, and took his position behind me.

Chapter 16

The campsite we had chosen was awe-inspiring. With the Winckenlaw Mountains behind us and the vast Plain of Mungreat stretching endlessly before our eyes, we found ourselves in the foothills of the same mountains, surrounded by lush and nearly untouched forests.

Not far away, the smoke from the Formorrid encampment could be seen rising, but thanks to the rise of the hills and the magic of the Drui, we remained hidden from their view.

Two days later, Alaric arrived, having skillfully circumvented the Formorrid camp to remain undetected. It was clear from his expression that he had successfully routed the other encampment.

"The Formorrid are gone," he announced, taking a sip of mead after changing from his travel clothes. "The ones on the island are all dead, as reported by my father's forces. The mages from the other camp are missing; we don't know if they are dead or simply gone. Some bodies bear no wounds, and it's a baffling sight. The Vikes don't use magic in battle; we rely on swords, spears, and occasional bows." His haunted eyes hinted at the sights he had witnessed.

"Well, the main thing is that they are gone from there," I replied. "We will be launching an attack against their camp in a day or so. The Drui and the Sidheran mages are currently deciding on the date and time."

"I don't fully understand all the details," I admitted. "It has something to do with the positions of the sun and moon and the advice of the Great Elementals. Labraird, Odine, Daman, and Mayveer are handling it. They seem to know what's going on. I'll simply follow their guidance. I feel that it's not just about me but my role as the Bearer of the Key Lifenstone. Your presence is important too, as 'male and female representatives of the Land must be present,' according to Labraird and Daman."

"Drui and Skaalds," Alaric laughed, "they are all alike. They think in symbols, not in concrete things. Well, they are the learned ones here. I am simply happy to be back with you, no matter what tomorrow brings." Saying this, he put down his cup and reached for my hand. "We live in perilous times, my love. But I have faith in both our people and in the Sidherans. We will prevail, and when the Formorrid threat is over, we will make this land glorious, the envy of all the world."

I chuckled nervously. "Let's hope not too glorious that we invite another empire to consider conquering us. I'd be content with our nations at peace, living in prosperity, hope, and honor."

Further conversation was interrupted by the entrance of my chief advisors through the tent flap.

"Tomorrow at Dawning," proclaimed Labraird as he strode in. "We will use the power of Light to overcome the Dark Tribe. The spirits of Air, Water, and Land will be with us. The Formorrid will face their worst fear, Elemental Light and Fire."

Labraird grinned, obviously pleased with his plan. Although I felt somewhat bewildered by the details, Mayveer sensed it and intervened.

"Labraird, hold your speech. Our ArdRighian may not grasp your words fully," she said. "Don't worry, niece. All will be made clear tomorrow. Tonight, Odine and Daman will guide you through some meditation before bedtime. In the morning, you'll know what to do. Trust in the Lifenstone, and follow your instincts, and all will be well."

I nodded, gesturing for them to take a seat and eat. Tomorrow promised to be a long, tiring, and eventful day. Little did I know then how right I would be.

The Bard and Skaald indeed led me through meditations that night, but I cannot recall the specifics. I only remember hearing songs in Vike, Eirlandian, and High Eirl as I lay in a small hut away from the camp's noise.

Vilk stood guard outside, along with Alaric and others. Labraird and Mayveer were likely finalizing the attack plans.

The next morning, darkness shrouded the surrounding area, with only a hint of light beyond the tent opening. Strange, but I quickly dismissed it as Alaric stirred beside me and opened his eyes.

"Blessings on you today," he said in Vike, the traditional words spoken before embarking on an adventure, trade, or war. "May the Forces be with you."

"May the Sword of Morrigan guard your back," I replied in Eirlandian, our saying to soldiers and sailors before battle.

Vilk came in with hot drinks and barley cakes. "You must eat, ArdRighian," he grinned. "The Bard Daman told me to ensure you drink all the tea. It has special herbs for strength and attunement to the greater Force, whatever that may mean."

I smiled back, feeling grateful for Vilk's presence and friendship. "Don't worry, I'll eat and drink my fill. I'm unsure when I'll get the chance again," I replied.

After breakfast, Alaric stepped outside to confer with the Drui and Skaald. I put on the special white robe left by Daman, embroidered with silver designs of protection and power. Daman explained it was of Sidheran make to safeguard me from Formorrid spells and prevent any backlash from my Lifenstone's power.

The Lifenstone was already warm as I took it off its chain and placed it into a wooden staff made of oak, wrapped with silver wire to secure a small gem holder. With the stone in place, I spoke the Words of Securing taught by Daman, and it became fused to the staff.

The ground was cool beneath my feet, but I had to remain barefoot to stay connected to the earth's energy.

Outside, Alaric and several others departed for the far end of the Formorrid camp, aiming to ambush any fleeing enemies. Eirlandian mages and Drui with battle magic powers joined them, while others took positions around the encampment.

The Formorrid would find themselves surrounded, though the fog that now enveloped the valley and their camp hid this fact. I realized that the fog was a product of weather magic from the Drui, concealing our forces until the right moment.

I joined Labraird, Odine, and Mayveer, with Vilk always attentive nearby. Labraird pointed to a hill before us, slightly to the right, which offered an advantageous view of the Formorrid encampment.

"We'll attack from there," he stated. "The four of us will set up a protective barrier. You'll stand in the middle and direct the Sacred Fire through the Lifenstone. Aim for the tents first to eliminate hiding places. Then call upon Greater Lightning to strike the leaders. The lightning will be drawn to their magic. Once the leaders are dealt with, we'll demand surrender. If they resist, we'll have to eliminate them all. We'll assist with the lesser Formorrid, but only you can breach their magical barrier to attack."

Odine added, "Don't underestimate the difficulty. They'll fight back, and we don't know their weapons or magic. The combined strength of your Lifenstone and the others will be enough to destroy what must be destroyed. Use the staff to direct the Power. Choose your targets wisely to minimize harm to the land."

I nodded, feeling my throat go dry. Discussing this in the privacy of my tent was one thing, but here, in the dim light of pre-dawn, the weight of what I was about to attempt hit me like a tidal wave.

Daman sensed my unease and took my hand, offering gentle counsel. "Do not dwell on this, Tara," he said soothingly. "You are merely the channel through which the energy flows. The Great Ones will guide you, and you should not feel ashamed of your actions. Today, you will perform great deeds that will be sung for generations, and the people will hail you as savior and rightful sovereign. The High Powers have decreed it, and they will make it happen. Fear not."

He handed me another cup. "Drink," he commanded. "This water comes from the Sacred Well of Liffey. It will be your only sustenance until your task is done, but its magical properties will grant you strength unlike any other drink or food." I drank the water, and it indeed made me feel better.

"Come," Mayveer said, taking my hand. "Ride with me. My steed is strong and can carry us both swiftly. We must reach the hill just before sunrise."

Mayveer's steed looked more like a war steed than a lady's mount, but it was gentle as I mounted without a saddle, just a blanket with straps. The reins seemed only for grip, as the steed knew where to go without guidance.

"Our steeds are different from yours," Mayveer explained. "They understand our needs without restraints or devices. He knows where we need to go and the quickest route. Hold onto me, and he will ensure we remain safe."

With that, she spoke a word in Sidheran, and the steed swiftly carried us through the woods and over streams. We reached our destination much faster than an Eirlandian steed could manage, even with a knowledgeable rider.

The hilltop was adorned with small stones bearing ancient carvings.

Symbols of our deities, power, strength, and storm were recognizable. These dolmens dotted the landscape of Eirlandia, remnants of a time beyond memory, when the first beings set foot on this land. Who they were and why they set these stones up remains a mystery. Some say it were the Formorrid, but most disregard that theory. The Lifenstone on my staff seemed to pulse with a gentle light, surrounded by a nimbus.

Mayveer asked me to dismount, and her command to the steed sent it off to a safe spot. "I don't wish to endanger any creature during this," she said. I agreed, looking for the best vantage point to observe the Formorrid encampment.

Mayveer pointed to a group of stones at the crown of the hill. "This is where you must stand," she said. "There's a stone to hold the staff, so you won't have to keep it upright yourself. You'll need to hold it, of course, but the stone will assist you and prevent the Master Lifenstone from being captured by magic."

I followed her directions, and the stone offered me a convenient place to position the staff. Closing my eyes, I conjured the image of Tarantitas, the god of Lighting and Keeper of the Sacred Fire. "Tarantitas, hear me," I whispered in the ancient tongue of Eirl. "Keeper of the Sacred Fire, light your hearth and send your torch. I, Tara, bearer of the Master Lifenstone, call upon you. Come to aid your people. Burn off the fog so we may strike."

A gasp from Mayveer made me open my eyes. The fog swiftly dissipated as shafts of lightning fell from a cloudless sky onto the Formorrid camp. Chaos erupted as they scrambled to understand what was happening. Although the shadows hid me from normal sight, I knew their magic could reveal my presence.

Gazing below, I spotted a menacing device in the middle of their camp. It looked unlike anything I'd seen before, and my heart pounded in fear. Mayveer warned me that it was the Eye of Ballor, a terrible machine of destruction. I knew I had to eliminate the operators before they could use it against us.

The Eye of Balor was known to any child of Eirlandia. Tales of its strange ability to both bring out great admiration and great fear in its presence was something learned at a young age. It had been believed the weapon destroyed in the Last Great War, but that obviously was not true. Mounted on a very large wooden frame, the Eye at this point looked like an enormous black boulder, polished and shaped to resemble an eye shut. But once the lid was lifted, the power contained within the device could bring total destruction upon any target it was set upon. Without the power of the Great Ones, the Formorrid would win this battle before it was even begun.

I was unsure if my Lifenstone was powerful enough to destroy this machine. I knew, intellectually, that it was linked to other stones, but I could not totally believe such thing. I had to have faith that the magic of the Sidheran, who had forged this and the other Lifenstones, was powerful enough to destroy an Eye of Balor. I had been told many times it was indestructible. How would only one Lifenstone, linked or not, be enough? Perhaps, I silently mused, I need only destroy the operators. Surely there cannot be that many among the Formorrid who had the knowledge and power to command the Eye.

"Send the Lightning of Justice upon them," I commanded the Lifenstone verbally, focusing on the five figures in black robes who approached the device.

A blinding beam of light shot out from the Lifenstone, dividing into separate beams that struck the five Formorrid, leaving only smoldering remains. With the camp ablaze, I took a moment to rest as Mayveer brought me more water.

Suddenly, a loud noise boomed from the camp. Mayveer crouched down, and I shouted something I can't recall, causing the staff to generate a protective shield around us. The Eye had activated, emitting a black cloud of destruction. The shield blocked its effects, and I heard the screams of rage from below.

"You at the top," a large figure dressed in red spoke up, wielding a staff with a black crystal at its top. "You cannot destroy this machine or the whole Formorrid contingent. One Lifenstone is not powerful enough. Surrender the false ArdRighian, Tara, and we will leave your island in peace. We don't quarrel with the Eirlandian people, or the Vikes, or even the Sidheran. We want only Tara, and we swear not to harm her. But she must not rule, for if she does, it is likely our race would perish." The figure paused for a moment, as if awaiting a reply. "I am called Borrmid, and I am a Greater Mage. I wield power you cannot hope to overcome. What is your answer?"

I remembered what Daman and the others had said. I was the Child of Prophecy, and my reign with Alaric would mark the start of the Formorrid's decline. 'One Lifenstone is not powerful enough,' the mage had said. Then I would have to gather more Lifenstones.

Concentrating on the unfamiliar words I had memorized, I called upon the Greater Ones and the Powers of Earth, Air, Fire, and Water to link the Lesser Lifenstones to mine, uniting their powers.

The strange words, which were in a language that resembled High Eirl, but were also different, echoed in my head and almost hurt my mouth to speak. I wondered briefly in one corner of my mind if these words were Sidheran, as I had never heard that language spoken. A wave of almost nausea went through me at that moment. Images of different stones flashed through my mind, along with quick pictures of those I assumed were the mages connected with the Lifenstones. I felt a heavy pressure around my heart for just a moment, then it withdrew and a feeling of calm and great strength superseded it. It was then I knew that all the Lifenstones were now connected.

I raised my voice and addressed the Formorrid. "It is I, the ArdRighian of Eirlandia, who speaks. Thank you for your words about the Eye of Balor, but my people will not surrender me. Instead, I offer you a chance to withdraw and refrain from interfering in this land or any other. If you accept, send your emissary to Kilawey to seek peace. Otherwise, I will bring the full force of my power upon you."

"Foolish girl," Borrmid, replied. "You'll regret leaving Vikland. I never trusted you when you were at my Dun, and I trust you even less now."

With his words I realized why I had felt the figure was familiar. If this was truly the same Borrmid, then I had reason to be very cautious and perhaps even a little afraid. Parts of my mind screamed warnings, but I gave no outward sign of the war of sensations within me.

I recalled Alaric's warnings about Borrmid and his interest in me. The thought that he might be the mastermind behind the Eye of Balor and other dangerous devices chilled me.

"You can't hope to win this battle," he taunted. "Your forces are being defeated in the field. Your Council will soon beg for terms."

With determination, I summoned the Lightning of Justice once more, channeling the combined power of all the Lifenstones. But nothing happened for a long moment. Unlike the first time, it seemed as if there was a counter-force fighting against me and the Lifenstone's power. Looking over at Borrmid, I realized his stone was blazing also and there was a not-quite-visible battle going on in the sky between us. Borrmid was, I realized, a very strong mage; and it occurred to me that he might not be the only one against whom I was fighting. Keeping all my will on the battle, I looked over again and narrowed my eyes against the glare suddenly coming from the Formorrid position. I realized the glare was from other stones, whose masters were sending their energy to reinforce Borrmid's stone and magic. Much the same as I had done with the Master Lifenstone, linking the Lesser Stones to the Master from a distance, Borrmid was doing the same at this very moment.

"Mayveer!" I called. "We need mages to take out the other Formorrid near Borrmid! He has help and is too strong with the back up!"

I did not hear a verbal answer, but felt a wave of reassurance.

A second or two later, I mentally received a message from Labraird. "Concentrate on keeping up the attack on the Eye. My Drui will take care of the mages in just a moment. Do not waiver, do not lose heart. This is the critical moment in this contest of wills. Borrmid hopes you haven't noticed his augmentation of mages and their stones. He knows that you can't prevail against all of them, as powerful as the Master Lifenstone is, it was not designed for this kind of use for any length of time. Therefore, you must let him THINK he is winning, so that he doesn't notice our attack until it is too late to stop it."

"Understood," I mentally replied. Shifting my weight, I closed my eyes and visualized all I had to lose if Borrmid won. I imagined my country in ruins, with Borrmid and his ilk sitting on the throne of the ArdRighian and ordering his men to find and kill all Drui in order to eliminate any possibility of resistance.

In the midst of those horrible mental scenes, I suddenly heard a horrendous sound of multiple instances of mental and physical anguish. I opened my eyes to behold at least a half dozen, perhaps more, pillars of fire where the other Formorrid mages had stood moments before. Obviously Labraird had been successful in his counter-attack.

A half second later, the bolt surged forth, and I felt an overwhelming surge of energy, as if the Divine Lightning flowed not just through the staff and Lifenstone, but also through me. The sensation was both exhilarating and terrifying.

Hours later, I would learn that my intuition was correct—I had indeed tapped into the power of the Divine Lightning, an experience I would never forget.

Chapter 17

I awoke back at our camp. The Lifenstone lay once again in its setting on my chest. Despite feeling drained, I also felt strangely whole and at ease. I turned my head and saw Alaric sitting a small distance away, studying a map. His tired but satisfied expression spoke of victory.

"We must have won," I said softly.

At the sound of my voice, Alaric looked over at me and smiled. "Indeed we did," he answered. "It was a near rout. You were much too busy with your own battle, but my men and I, along with a veritable army of Drui and Fighdrui mages fought off the Formorrid successfully. It was not easy, nor particularly quick, but I have seen enough mage-battle now to last me the rest of my lifetime. I'm not used to such goings on. Give me a clean physical battle any day over watching people suddenly burst into flame, or crumble to dust, or seem to be hit by a thousand, invisible arrows, and the gods know what else those mages did that I didn't witness!"

"What of the mages and the Emissary, what of the Eye?" I asked anxiously.

"All that remains of the Eye of Balor, Emissary Borrmid, and his team can be carried away by a small horse cart," Alaric answered as he stepped towards me. "As for the other troops, I doubt the clean-up crew will find anything left to do." He walked over and took a seat where he could hold my hand. "We have won a great victory, and our losses were minimal."

Alaric bent down and looked deeply into my eyes. "I was frightened for you, Little Eaglet. I did not know what was happening, and when I saw that lightning on the hill I almost thought my heart was going to come right out of my throat, so hard was it hammering." He bent down and kissed me quickly, but I could feel he was warring in himself against the need to do much more.

"As you can see, my Vike, all is well. I worried for you also, but I had faith that the Old Ones would see you safe and returned to me."

"Now, however," said Alaric in a strange tone of voice, "I have just been told that a great challenge still awaits us. Well, awaits you, actually."

My eyebrow quirked at this. "What great challenge?" I asked. "I have yet to fully take up ruling. What more is there to do that I don't already know about?"

"You must create anew the Crowns of Eirlandia," Labraird answered as he entered the tent. I looked askance at him, wondering if he had overheard my question.

"In ages long past, the ArdRigh and Righian wore special crowns with powers to keep the land united and to protect against the Formorrid and the Vikes," he continued. "Obviously, the Vikes are no longer a threat and are, indeed, our allies. The crowns would ensure their loyalty and secure Eirlandia against any future dealings with the Formorrid or other unknown nations that might pose a threat.

"The old crowns were lost or destroyed," he continued as he took a seat near Alaric, "no one knows which, in one of the last battles of the last Formorrid Conflict. The Sidheran mages have indicated they stand ready to help create new crowns, as does Skaald Odine and, of course, the Drui that have this sort of knowledge. The materials are being gathered and prepared as we speak. But the power of the Lifenstones will be needed to complete the work. The sooner we can do this, the sooner we can breathe easier, knowing our future is secured."

"I am strong enough to travel," I replied, sitting up to prove it. "When can we leave?"

Alaric looked askance at me, and Labraird glowed. Just then the door opened again, and Skaald Odine entered. "Ah, Tara, I see you have recovered. And from the look on Labraird's face, I would say you have learned of the new task and wish to get started on it as soon as possible."

I nodded. "I am well. I wish this done so we can get on with our lives."

"Indeed," he agreed. "Spoken as a true ArdRighian and leader. It is late now, but we can leave in the morning. The Sidherans have agreed to let you travel, by closed litter, through their kingdom back to Kilawey. It is safer and much easier. Once there, the good mages, the Drui, and myself will finish the work on the crowns and determine the best date for their infusion with the Master Lifenstone's power. Do not worry; all will be done soon."

"Let us hope so, Skaald," Alaric answered. "I am not used to all the magic. Give me a foe that fights with bow and spear and axe, and I shall be there. But ones who use strange machines and magics beyond my reckoning, well, that is another matter."

We spent one more night at camp. It was in the quiet hours after all had retired that Alaric and I again had space and privacy to discuss what had happened that day.

We lay together on furs which covered a good-sized straw mattress. By unspoken arrangement, all seemed to know we needed to spend the night together.

Alaric lay on his side, one arm pillowing his head while the other stroked my hair gently. This was a habit he had started in Vikland and which he did whenever he or I, or both of us, had had a trying day. I silently agreed with his assessment of the day and smiled up at him gratefully.

"I was so worried, my heart," he said to me in Vik. "I didn't want to be separated from you, but I knew that I would only be in the way and that my battle skills were needed to deal with the soldiers of the Formorrid. They were quite formidable, by the way," he spoke matter-of-factly, with more than a touch of admiration in his voice. "I may not like the race, but I cannot deny their battle prowess."

"My warrior mate," I teased gently. "I think Vikes are born with weapons in their hands."

"No," he answered, "but our first toys are usually miniature axes." He smiled and leaned over to kiss me.

"I DID worry about you," I confided. "But it was locked up in a small corner of my brain. I couldn't spare you my full attention.

Bormmid and his Eye of Balor almost defeated me, and that would have meant both my death and the death of the entire nation."

I shuddered then, thinking how close I had come to being defeated.

Alaric shifted and placed his hand over my heart. "I promise you, my dear one, that I will never again let you be alone if you must put yourself in such danger again."

"You won't have a choice," I told him gently. "Some things must take place in ways you can never understand. But, believe me, I was not alone. I could feel your love and thoughts even though we were miles away. It has been so for some time, and I know it will be so until we die. Even then, I feel we will not be long parted, even if you should go to the Halls of your gods and I go to mine,"

"Enough talk," Alaric said suddenly. Reaching over to where a lamp burned, he switched it off and then pulled me to him.

Without another spoken word, we two took comfort in each other and reveled in the fact we were alive, healthy and young. The power of love is a great one, and we soon had spent our passions, and drifted off to sleep, still wrapped in each other's arms.

The next morning, Alaric and I traveled by litter through part of the Realm of the Sidheran. While I learned later that Mayveer traveled with us, and was, indeed, our guide, we heard no sound and no one spoke to us or anyone else.

After a length of time that I cannot state, we came out again into sunlight, and the door of the litter was opened.

Before us, just down a small slope, lay Kilawey. Seeing the town and then the royal quarters, I was filled with relief but also dread. I had no idea how I was going to create something I had never seen even pictures of, much less learn the skills needed for such an undertaking.

I had little time to panic, however, as we were escorted without comment through a doorway that appeared suddenly before us, and we found ourselves in the Great Hall, in a small, unlit alcove. The Sidheran guard saluted me and Alaric and then turn and entered the doorway again. Said doorway suddenly disappeared, leaving a blank wall.

Looking at Alaric, I simply shrugged, indicating my lack of knowledge and the two of us went swiftly to our quarters. We had returned victorious, but there was now another daunting task awaiting us.

At the Night of the Moon's Fullness, Labraird, Odine, and Daman again entered the royal court and bade me change into a gown of white and accompany them, along with Alaric, to the Sacred Grove.

Upon arrival, I saw fourteen cowled figures, each one a color that stood for one of the Tribes of Eirlandia, along with empty places for Odine as the representative of Vike, Daman as the representative of the Bards, and for myself and Alaric. A large white stone stood in the center of the circle of people, and upon it were two covered forms, which I assumed were the crowns.

Labraird went to the east side of the stone and gestured for us to stand on the west side. My Lifenstone began to warm, and I quickly brought it out so that it rested upon my clothes. Labraird smiled slightly in what seemed to be satisfaction, then faced both Alaric and me, with a faraway look in his eyes, as if he saw something just above and behind us that neither of us could see.

"I summon the Greater Ones, the Protectors, the Spirits of the Ancestors of this land, Eirlandia," he began in High Eirl, the language of magic and antiquity. "I invoke the Three-Fold Way and the Five-Fold Treasures of Life. For the love of this land, for its safety and continuance, we give both thanks and ask for a blessing. Set your power, Oh Mighty Ones, into these tokens of Rule. May these crowns ensure the lasting peace and prosperity of Eirlandia and her allies."

He took off the cloth that had hidden the crowns. I remember I gasped slightly in wonder. Made of a material I was later to learn was almonite, the crowns were decorated with small gems of varying kinds, with a Lifenstone placed high and center in the more elaborate of the crowns.

I understood which crown was for whom then; the larger crown being for the actual ArdRigh or ArdRighian, and the smaller, less elaborate crown for the consort.

Their cunning design made them adjustable to the size of the person wearing it. These crowns would never be too small or too large; they would never require adjustment in any way. They were works of wonder and of such craftsmanship as I had never before seen.

"ArdRighian Tara of Eirlandia," intoned Labraird formally, "take your Lifenstone and place it on top of the Lifenstone that is on your crown." I followed his instructions and placed the two stones facing each other.

"Now concentrate on your stone and will its power to flow into and be shared by this new Lifenstone," he commanded.

I closed my eyes, and saw the two Lifenstones before me. "Heed my words," I said silently in Eirl to my old Lifenstone. "Share your power, stone of my mother and her people. Link yourself to it as you are linked with all the others of your ilk. Share your power, but be not diminished."

I felt my command take hold, and a feeling of power washed over me and went to the crown. A moment later, the power returned to me, feeling different yet whole and strengthened.

"It is done," decreed Labraird. I opened my eyes and saw that the Lifenstone in the crown now also glowed, as did my own. "Take your first stone, ArdRighian, and place it upon the consort's crown." Labraird ordered. "It too must be linked. It bears a much smaller stone and less power, but it is not without power itself, for at times the Consort must rule and have the power to protect the land in the place of the ArdRigh or ArdRighian."

I did as commanded and placed the Lifenstone at the top of the crown. This time it was Labraird who commanded the stone, speaking in a language I did not know. The Lifenstone blazed again, and the consort's crown sparkled in a dazzling display of light. In a few moments, all was again quiet.

I glanced over at Alaric, who was eyeing the crown with a mixture of speculation and reluctance. Without command, I retrieved my Lifenstone and placed it around my neck once more, letting it stay in full view.

"The Blessings of the Northern Ones be upon these crowns and those who wear them," proclaimed ArdSkaald Odine into the silence. "Ever shall Vikland be a friend to Eirlandia, as long as the rightful rulers wear these crowns."

Each person in the circle also gave their blessings in the name of the tribe or group they represented. At the end of it, Labraird came around to our side of the altar and gestured for us to step back a bit. Upon impulse, I got down on one knee. Labraird looked at me strangely, then smiled, just a little, and gave a little nod. Whatever had prompted me, it seems it had been the correct thing to do.

Labraird lifted first the Consort Crown and turned to Alaric, who hastily followed my example when he realized what was about to happen.

"Do you swear, Prince Alaric of Vikland, consort of Tara, ArdRighian of Eirlandia, to faithfully perform your duties of Consort for the protection and preservation of this land, before all others?" asked Labraird in a ringing voice, meant to carry to all three worlds, I believed.

"I so swear," answered Alaric. "As I love your ArdRighian, so do I love this land, and I swear to protect both of them for as long as I have the capability." Labraird smiled and placed the crown on Alaric's head.

"Long and fruitful may be your life and reign, Prince Consort Alaric," he proclaimed.

Then he turned back to the stone and lifted the Ruler's Crown above my head. "Do you swear, ArdRighian Tara, once of Kilbrae and now of all Eirlandia, to faithfully perform your duties as ArdRighian of Eirlandia for as long as the people and Forces of Eirlandia deem it?"

"I so swear," I answered. "I never asked for or dreamt of this day, but I will defend and rule my land in justice and equality, with sword and with magic for as long as my people want me and the Spirits give me the power."

With those words, the Ruling Crown was placed upon my head, and I suddenly knew the full meaning of my words and my life. I was Eirlandia, and She was me, and together we would strive to be the best we could be.

Chapter 18

Maeve

Maeve looked up from her reading and was astonished, for the day was almost gone. She wouldn't even have time to start out before she would be forced to camp for the night.

"What is it about this book," she wondered, "that so catches me up in it that I lose all track of time? It is not in the nature of Fighdrui to be so fixated on one thing." She had read a great deal of the book, but there was much left, and she was running out of time. She still knew nothing of what happened to the Master Lifenstone and the Crowns. Part of her urged her to simply bring the book to court and let the scholars take over, but the selfish side of her whispered that maybe it was the Elder Ones' will that she be one to find the Master Lifenstone and to bring it back with her.

The autumn had come, and winter storms would be starting soon. There would be no travel to Vikland or anywhere else for several months. Her task had been to find the book and return it. But once again, in Kilawey, she would be prevented from going back out to find the Master Lifenstone. She had to determine if the book mentioned the Master Lifenstone again and where it might be, for she somehow knew that the former Tara's Lifenstone was the key to finding the crowns.

Sighing, she marked the book with a scrap of paper and got up. Slowly stretching, she realized she had not eaten all day, so she prepared herself a simple meal from the store of food she had brought. The day was ending, and the light was fading, so she lit a solitary lamp and laid out her bedding. Luckily, there were spare blankets here, so she would not be cold, even though she would refrain from lighting a fire. Maeve thought back to her time of leaving Kilawey and her last conversation with Aelfund the night before.

Aelfund was the head of her order but also a dear friend who had known her since girlhood. It was unknown how old he actually was, as he didn't appear to age as other men. Still strong, red-haired, and in prime fighting condition, he could be 30, 40, 50 or even older. His outfit of close-fitting trews and shirt showed exactly how physically fit he was. His face was only lightly lined, and some whispered he had Sidheran blood that helped him stay young. Maeve didn't know if that was true or not, but in any case, he was someone you wanted on your side in any sort of battle, whether it be physical or mental.

"You know I do not wish to send you alone on this mission, Maeve," Aelfund had told her. "But the Chief Skaald and the ArdDrui have both told me that only you would have any chance of success in this endeavor. It seems that your genealogy makes you the best candidate for this task. They also both mentioned that not only the Crowns should be found, but the Master Lifenstone of the ArdRighian also. Hopefully, the book will hold the answers to both these mysteries.

"Finding the book is your first task," he had continued. "If you need extra time to follow other leads you may come across once you find the journal, you must let me know by Sending. We need it before the end of the harvest season to have enough time to search through it and find what we need to mount an expedition to retrieve the crowns and, hopefully, the Master Lifenstone.

"But until then, there is no hurry. Use your judgement; I trust you in this. And don't be afraid to call for backup if you need it. Go with my blessings and those of the Old Ones, Maeve. There is more riding on your success than you may understand." Maeve had nodded her understanding of his instructions and gone out, wondering what he had meant about her genealogy. She did not know much of her family line; few Fighdrui did. Now she wondered if, by chance, she had Sidheran blood, and that was why the Lifenstone seemed so important to her.

Well, it hardly mattered at this moment, she decided. She would skip even further in the book and try to find the section where Tara began speaking of hiding the crowns and perhaps the Master Lifenstone.

From reading the book, at least she understood the importance of the Master Lifenstone. While she had heard the term before, she knew only a few Lifenstones existed and that their powers were fairly limited. The ArdRighian had possession of one, but it was not Tara's Stone. Instead, it was the one that had belonged to Labraird, the ArdDrui of first Tara's reign.

Making herself some tea, Maeve sat back down and, again, prayed to the Elder Gods for guidance. She slipped the paper out of the book and then dug her fingers toward the end of the volume.

Surely, the final days of the Great Revolt would be recorded in the book, and in reading the days before their deaths, Maeve would find the references she needed. In the morning, she would do a Sending, telling Aelfund of her success in finding the book and telling him she was pursuing knowledge of the Lifenstone and would be delayed in returning.

She would also Send that she needed more supplies and was taking what was at the Waystation so that Aelfund would send someone out with more supplies. The waystations of the Fighdrui were never left bare except for emergencies and were always restocked as soon as possible.

As before, Maeve skimmed pages, skipping whole sections once she figured out the time involved. The years of Tara and Alaric's reign were good years for Eirlandia. The power of the Formorrid had been broken, and the treaty with the Vikes held strong and firm. King Leeife died of old age, and Alaric became King of the Vikes as well as Prince Consort of Eirlandia.

He appointed Skaald Odine as Chancellor, and Skaald went back to Vikland to rule in Alaric's stead. The two monarchs visited Vikland often, and Sven was named Heir and Chancellor after Skaald Odine's death. The guard Vilk became head of the Armed Forces of Vikland and also became Sven's best friend and comrade.

The ArdDrui Labraird died of an illness, and Culluchan took his place. "Ah," thought Maeve, "I am getting close then." She knew that Culluchan had not been ArdDrui long when the Great Revolt started, that unforeseen rising of some of the heads of the tribes against Tara and Alaric.

It had been found out after the fact that the Formorrid had infiltrated those courts and, through their potions and magics, had taken over the wills of those Righs who revolted, but the damage to the country had been done, and a new line of ArdRighs was established since Tara and Alaric had had no direct heirs. Maeve read with tears in her eyes as the ArdRighian revealed that she and Alaric would have no heir, for the magic she had wielded in order to create the Ruling Crowns had stopped her monthly courses, never to be resumed.

Still, the cousin whom the Sidheran had produced had been a good king, and his line had ruled Eirlandia well for many generations. The Vikes had had their own new king, of course, in Sven, but relations between the two countries stayed strong for some time before the Formorrid again worked their dark ways and turned the sentiments of the Vikes against the Eirlandians once again, although no war between the nations was ever fought.

Now, once again, the tide was turning, and the present King of Vikland was said to be considering asking for the hand of the ArdRighian in marriage, with the intent of once again combining the rule of Vikland and Eirlandia. Maeve could not help but wonder at the coincidence that these two rulers bore again the names of the first two joint rulers.

King Alaric II of Vikland and ArdRighian Tara Secunda of Eirlandia had met in a neutral nation a few years ago to sign a Declaration of Peace between the two nations. It had appeared to those present, Maeve being one of them, that the two had almost seemed to know each other, even though they had never met. The mutual attraction was obvious to all present, and it came as no surprise this last Spring when

King Alaric had formally requested the hand of Tara in marriage and assured her of his intent to be only her consort in Eirlandia as she would be his in Vikland. The only caveat to this proposal was the stipulation that the Ruling Crowns be found and the couple re-coronated on their wedding day as joint rulers of Eirlandia and Vikland.

The crowns bore Lifenstones, she knew, but the Master Lifenstone had been separated and held the key, she was sure, to the success of the finding of the Crowns.

Maeve sipped her tea and turned the pages, scanning quickly. She didn't need anything before the time, just before the Last Battle, when the Royal Consort and the ArdRighian had lost their lives. She knew they had hidden the crowns just before then and, she assumed, the Master Lifenstone also. If they had had those objects, perhaps the battle would not have been lost. Had the battle gone differently, then the nation's whole history could have changed. However, Maeve knew the crowns and the Master Lifenstone had been taken out of play, as the future had not been assured. Tara and Alaric wanted to ensure the objects were safe from discovery by the enemy. For example, had the objects fallen into the hands of the Formorrid, Maeve was sure that her country would not still exist.

Maeve skipped even further ahead. She was close to the end of the book now, but not too close. She knew she needed a few weeks or more before the battle. She wasn't sure when ArdRighian Tara last wrote in the book or even if the last entries were by someone else, and she resisted the temptation to go to the very end and find out. She scanned quickly and read snatches regarding the start of the rebellion and the loss of lives on both sides.

"It seems our time here is almost done," Maeve read. "The council has fled, many turning from me and Alaric, victims of the lies that have been spread about us. Soon, we will have to fight our own people, and my heart grows heavy at the thought. I will not use the Master Lifenstone against my own. It will be sent away, where it can do no harm and where, perhaps, it will be found again by another ruler and used to again right wrongs in another time."

"At last," Maeve breathed. "Tell me, Tara, where did you send the precious stone?"

Chapter 19

I detest the thought of civil war, and I will not kill those who come unless I have no choice.

For this reason, I am hiding away the Master Lifenstone. I do not want to be tempted to use its power against my own people. Tonight, I will make a journey such as never before.

I will go with my mother's sister to the Forbidden Realm, the heart of the Sidhe, where only the Master Mages are usually allowed. I go to bring the Sidheran the greatest treasure in this land and to ask their help in concealing the second greatest treasures, our crowns.

I do not wish either the Master Lifenstone or the Ruling Crowns to be worn by those who come after us until such time as Alaric and I again walk this earth and can again take up the crowns to continue this work which we have begun.

That Alaric and I will live again has already been foretold in the prophecy Labraird and I discussed years ago. The same prophecy that told of my birth and rise to power spoke also of the fact that I would come again, and would my life mate. I know we live in a cycle of lives, and I know that our lives are not yet over. We have ruled and lived a good time in this cycle, but there are still things to be done, and even if this war had not come, we could not have lived long enough to do it all. Nor could all that we wish for both Eirlandia and Vikland have been possibly accomplished in one short lifetime. No, the Great Ones understand that some things need more than one life to accomplish. I know that Alaric and I will live again on some distant day, but I hope that we will again come together so that the work we have begun here will not take too long to be finished.

I know where I will place the Master Lifenstone. How I will do this deed is what I do not know. Mayveer says none but a full Sidheran has ever walked in the Forbidden Realm, and even the Master Mages do so at great peril and only in great need, for the ways of the Forbidden Realm are not our ways.

But this will be the safest place in all the realms for the Master Lifenstone, so great is its magic and power. I am frightened, for while I will visit the Sidheran realm in my body, I will not physically visit the Forbidden Realm. Only in the spirit may I walk the paths of that place, and how I will place a physical object somewhere while incorporeal, I have no idea. I can only assume the Mages know the way of this since they have agreed to help me.

The writing stopped there, and Maeve swore the spots on the page were the remains of tears. Turning the page, she read on.

I am dressed in the simplest of gowns. I wear no jewelry except the Master Lifenstone upon my breast. It lies quiet now, but I still can feel its hidden power. Looking up from this journal, I see Alaric at the window. His face is drawn and pale. He does not wish me to undertake this journey. He does not understand why I must do this.

We spoke long into the night last night, and I know he still isn't satisfied with my answers and reasons, but I have no more to tell him. This is something I simply know and cannot fully explain. I do not worry, really, about being lost in the Forbidden Realm, as seers greater than I have already foretold the manner of our deaths. We will die together, back-to-back, and we will be the agents of our own deaths, for we will call upon powers we would normally transmit through the Master Lifenstone or Crown straight through ourselves, for only in that way will we be able to save the land from total destruction.

The exact way of it is yet unknown, but I know when I die, it will not be tonight in the Realm of the Sidheran but will, instead, be in the bright light of day and on the Hill of Kincordia.

Again, the page ended abruptly, and Maeve turned to the next entry.

I have done what must be done and, since I still live, will tell now how this deed was accomplished.

When the door was opened, I saw Alaric, Daman, Mayveer and Culluchan standing in the hallway. Like myself, Mayveer was dressed very simply. For the first time, I realized that she, too, owned a Lifenstone, for it hung in plain sight on her gown, blazing brightly. Her hair was drawn up and away from her face for the first time also, and I saw the point to her ears that marked her Sidheran more than any other physical feature.

Alaric, Daman, and Culluchan would, I knew, accompany me only as far as the chamber in the Sidheran realm where my body would lie while my spirit journeyed with the Stone to the Forbidden Realm.

Mayveer, on the other hand, would travel with me, for she was only one of a few who knew the ways of that place and the only one who would agree to lead me. I had been told the other Sidheran mages were reluctant to allow this, but she was a Principia, a powerful Mage and my aunt, all of which carried much weight in the High Council. So it had been decided that I be allowed this since the hiding away of the Master Lifenstone was something all wished accomplished, and, in the end, all agreed that the Forbidden Realm was the best place to do it.

Mayveer actually smiled, which put me somewhat at ease. "Do not be frightened, my sister's daughter," she said in Eirl. "The way is not so terrible, and I will be there to guide you. No harm will come to you, although you will feel weak for a while afterwards both because of the journey and also because you will no longer have the strength of the Lifenstone with you to call upon at need."

Her words, although meant to reassure, I'm sure, sent a chill through my soul. I somehow suddenly realized just what amount of power I was about to give up. But I knew it had to be done, for sake of Eirlandia. I could not let the power of the Lifenstone fall into the wrong hands.

"Tara, my Love," said Alaric, "take my arm and let us go. My soul is chilled with the thoughts of what you do tonight, but I know all will be well, and I understand the reasons for it. I and Daman and Culluchan will guard you with physical and magical means, although I certainly expect no attack, especially not in Sidhera."

I took my love's hand, then, and smiled at him. No matter what happened, I knew Alaric would be faithful and would protect me. I had no fear of dying that night. I knew I would survive; I only hoped

I would survive whole in mind, body and spirit, for no one had ever attempted what I was now set to do.

We travelled first through normal, well-lit corridors. I knew the Nemed well and thought I knew all of its secrets by now. But I was shown wrong. We came to a wall that I thought at first was a wrong turning, a dead end, but Mayveer held up her Stone and spoke some sort of phrase that opened the wall. What I mean by that is that the wall just seemed to disappear completely. There was no sound, no movement of the Stone. It was simply there one moment and replaced by a corridor leading onward into darkness in another.

"And that which is hidden is revealed for the Prophesied One," she told me in High Eirl as we passed through. "Remember that phrase. Commit it to memory. You must pass this saying down through the ages, so your successor will know it. And so I did, and I write the translation here. My successor will know High Eirl and so know the first of the passwords is passed.

As we walked, I realized that Mayveer's Stone was sending out enough light to easily see by, although it was a strange blue-tinged light. The walls here were only rough Stone and dirt, more of a tunnel than any finished corridor. Cool breezes touched my cheek on occasion, and I almost felt as if soft hands touched me from time to time.

Alaric shivered and held me closer. A soft, insistent murmuring occurred in my head, and I felt they were telling me something, but I didn't understand what. I somehow knew, however, that these were the voices of my ancestor Sidherans, who had come to guide and protect me on my journey.

I cannot say why I think that, but in light of the fact that I was spared some of the terrible visions I had heard could happen in the Forbidden Realm, I can only assume I was somehow protected.

A glance at Alaric's white face told me that he, however, was not protected and was probably experiencing some unpleasant sensations.

"It is alright, my Love," I murmured in Vike. "They are but shades of beings long gone and cannot hurt you. They have come to protect me and surely see you as no threat. Be at ease; these are not like your Vikland demons, who haunt the hidden passes in winter, ready to ensnare the unwary. Be at ease, for you walk with the one whom these spirits seek to protect."

I felt his hand unclench a little then and knew he had taken my words to heart. Behind me, I heard the other two men murmuring in low tones, but I could make out none of the words. I don't think they were conversing but were; instead, each saying prayers and chants of protection against whatever the Sidheran ancestors were doing to them.

"Be at ease, oh my worthy predecessors," I said in Eirl softly. "These men travel with me for my protection. Do them no harm." With my words, it seemed the forces withdrew, for the atmosphere immediately became less charged and fearful.

Mayveer looked back and smiled approvingly. "The Ancestors are pleased," she said. "You thought of the others besides yourself. You have passed the test and have been shown worthy to enter the Forbidden

Realm. We are almost at the outer chamber. Come, all of you; warmth and light and refreshment await us."

With that, we all hurried forward that much faster and, turning a corner, found ourselves in a somewhat large cavern. It was obviously natural, but steam issued from several small vents and couches and tables with food and drink were evident, as were glowing lights, the like of which I had seen only in the Formorrid Dun.

As if she could read my mind, Mayveer addressed the subject of the lights. "These may look familiar to you, Alaric and Tara. The Formorrid stole this secret of the lights from us in the Last Great War. It is a small enough thing, and we do not begrudge them.

In fact, much of what we have and have developed we would have shared freely with the Formorrid, but they chose to disbelieve us and tried to take what they wanted by force. They came away with precious little, but the knowledge of the lamps was one of their small victories."

Her light extinguished itself, and she led us to a smaller chamber that held two couches. Between the beds was a sitting chair, and small tables were on either side. Mayveer chose the bed on her right and sat down, taking off her Lifenstone and placing it on the table next to the bed. She indicated the other bed to me with a nod of her head.

"Lay yourself down, Tara, and remove the Lifenstone from the chain around your neck, but hold it firmly in your hands. Place the Stone so it rests on your chest, and your hands cover it." As I did as she commanded, she continued.

"Alaric, you and Daman go into the outer chamber for just a bit. ArdDrui Culluchan and I must prepare Tara, and then she and I must begin our journey. When Culluchan is satisfied we are on our way, he will come to tell you so you may come and watch over us."

Alaric came to me and bent down, kissing me fiercely. "Do not get yourself killed, Tara," he said in Vike, "or I swear I will come looking for you on the other side and damned be those that try to stop me." "I will not die here, Alaric," I assured him. "We yet have our final destinies to fulfill."

"I am not sure I believe your visions," he told me. "But if you promise me you will live, I will take that vow and hold you to it, Wooeden as my witness."

"I promise," I answered. "Now go, for the sooner this is done, the sooner we can return home and to our marriage bed." I grinned wickedly and winked.

Alaric laughed softly. "Ever my little Eaglet, aren't you?" he murmured as he strode through the entryway.

Mayveer laughed softly. "Alright, sister's daughter, now relax and close your eyes. Try to form the picture of the Lifenstone in your mind and hold it there. You will feel, probably, many strange sensations, but do not open your eyes, speak, or even move until I tell you. What Culluchan and I do here has never been done, and I can only hope that the Ancestor Spirits will guide and help us, for we will surely fail without them."

I closed my eyes and imagined the Master Lifenstone as I had seen it that morning on the hilltop against the Formorrid, blazing with light. I cannot describe adequately what, exactly, I felt. The sensation was almost one of falling, but I knew with a piece of my mind that I was still in the bed in the chamber deep underground, and there was nowhere to fall. Sensation seemed to desert me at one point, except for my hands, which I could still feel were tightly clutched around the Lifenstone.

Murmurs again sounded, but they seemed a chorus of voices, almost of the sea in a cave, whispering its age-old secrets to rocks. Then the sound almost of a waterfall, a roaring, deep sound that almost enveloped me, and then all was deathly still and quiet.

"Open your eyes, Tara, and gaze upon the Forbidden Realm." I heard Mayveer say. "We have done it; now we must reach the central well and return here in the allotted time, or we shall perish here, and our bodies be empty shells for as many days as it takes to starve." Those words shocked my eyes open. The first thing I saw was Mayveer, only not Mayveer. She was as beautiful as ever, only more, and she had a luminous cloud around her, and she seemed almost translucent.

"Whaa?" I started to say.

"You see my spirit, Niece," she said in answer to my unfinished word. "You are the same, although you will seem the same to yourself, for we can never see our own spirit in the same manner as others do. You still hold the Master Lifenstone; you must let it guide you now to its resting place. This was where it was created, and it will know how to get to the Sacred Well the best.

Hold it up. Its light will guide us now."

I took the Master Lifenstone and held it as she commanded. The light made a beam that crossed the space above us and showed a distant place that looked something like a tower.

"Good," declared Mayveer. "Now, command the Master Lifenstone to keep the tower lit but to light our way through the labyrinth. Do it silently. The Master Lifenstone will hear you and remember to speak in High Eirl."

I did as she commanded, and a second beam showed out from the Stone, lighting the path before us. "The beam will show us where to go. If we come to a crossroads, it will light the turning we must take," I told Mayveer, sure of my knowledge, even though I knew not where the knowledge came from.

"Then let us start off," she responded. "We will not need to eat, drink, or rest here, and you will find we will travel more swiftly than in our bodies. We can also cross places that would not be possible in physical form. But we still have long to travel and hazards to overcome between here and there.

All travel in the Forbidden Realm is a test of our inner selves, and the spirits of this place have no mercy on those whose inner strength is not great enough for the challenge." Those ominous words ringing in my ears, we took off at a lively pace, letting the beam guide us.

Even as I write these words, the specifics of this journey begin to fade. I remember thinking that the colors of the trees and sky were strange and somehow almost wrong. It seemed the leaves were silver and pink and purple, not the shades of green or even orange or red of any tree in Eirlandia.

I know that we turned left at the first crossing and came to a mighty river. Here, we had to simply 'will' ourselves across, but I swear I could feel the rushing spray on my face, and I felt cold and wet for some time afterwards.

The path did not run in a straight line but was fairly straightforward for some ways. The second turning was marked by what appeared to be an ancient oak. Here, we followed a line of trees, oak, ash, thorn, elder, birch and others, all the sacred trees, to a grove. These trees, unlike the others, were of a normal color, and I wondered if they were the ancestors of our sacred trees. It seemed wrong to ask such a question here, so I kept silent.

The grove was empty, and we saw our path almost straight across from where we entered. But getting there was not as easy as it seemed. Shades of the dead came to us, asking questions, trying to impede us, and setting traps that we had to avoid without losing too much time.

One such spirit was that of an old woman. Dressed in gray from head to toe, and wearing a shimmering veil that hid all but vague outlines of her face, she stood at the top of a small rise. Trees and bushes crowded close to the path on either side, and I knew there would be no going around her or pushing through her.

"Where do you go, Wanderers?" she asked, her strong voice at odds with her appearance.

"We travel with the acceptance and permission of the Old Ones," Maeve replied before I could summon an answer. "Leave us so that we may complete the task for which we have come."

"And what task would that be?" the being queried. "Mortals do not come here without good reason. I would know your reason and this task."

Maeve looked at me and nodded. It seemed I must be the one to answer the query.

"I am Tara of Eirlandia. My mother was Sidheran, I come by right of blood. We must entrust a powerful magical artifact to the Powers of this Realm," I answered. "Do not seek to delay us. The future of this realm, and that of Sidhera and Eirlandia depend upon the completion of this task, without delay."

"So you say," the spirit sneered. "What proof have you? What artifact do you bring to this realm?"

Wordlessly I held out the Master Lifenstone, so she could see it.

"Aaah!" she shrieked. "You bring such as THAT here?   B   e warned, Mortals, such as this cannot stay forever within this place."

"This we know," answered Mayveer. "It stays for only its allotted time, which the Old Ones will make known to us in their own season." With this the spirit faded away and we were free to continue. I would have wished this encounter was the only one, but it was not so. Without Mayveer, I do not know if I could have surmounted this test, for one of visions was an encounter with my brother, who had died in that terrible Vike raid so many years ago. This encounter is too painful even now to recount. Let me say only that this version of my father and brother were of sides of them I had never seen in life, for they were full of vindictiveness and blamed me for their deaths. I can only believe they were malevolent spirits who took on the semblance of my loved ones in order to torment me better.

Finally, we reached the other side and headed back into a wooded area, which led up to higher ground. We could not see what lay ahead, but Mayveer kept urging me to hurry, saying she felt we were almost there and that our time was running out.

Topping a rise, we suddenly saw the tower and the large Well in front of it. There appeared to be no more impediments, and we ran down the hill into the glen. The Master Lifenstone was blazing now, literally pulling me forward. At the edge of the Well was a case of almonite and silver, the top already open. A deep cushion of felt was inside and I gently laid the Master Lifenstone within. The light dimmed to almost nothing, but then I noticed that the tower appeared to gleam with its own light, so we were not left in darkness. I closed the case and looked at Mayveer, unsure what to do next.

"Consign the case and Master Lifenstone to the Well of Life. It will not be harmed. As you drop it, tell the Well who it must next allow to retrieve the Master Lifenstone, lest it remain here forever. Do this silently, for even I must not know what limits and conditions you put upon this so that I am not tempted, in some future life, to come back and try to retrieve it myself."

As she commanded, I told the Well whom next it must allow retrieve the case and its contents. I cannot write this down, but I swear that The One Who Is To Come will know the words, pass the Forbidden Realm tests and retrieve the Lifenstone at the correct time and place. Once the case and Master Lifenstone were out of sight, I turned to Mayveer. "We no longer have a guide; how do we get out in time?" She smiled knowingly. "The way out is much easier than the journey within," she said. "Come, let us climb the opposite hill, and you will see what I mean."

We journeyed up the hill, and, to my amazement, there, just a short distance away, was the door that led into the chamber where Mayveer and I, in our physical forms, rested.

We walked to the door, slid through and looked upon our sleeping forms. Alaric was seated beside me and Culluchan beside Mayveer, both keeping vigil.

"Watch what I do," said Mayveer. "I have taken this journey a few times before. Coming back is not hard, but it can be disorienting. Do not worry if you feel very tired when your physical body awakes. Drink and eat, even though you will not want to. You will feel better quickly."

Then she walked to her body and climbed into the bed, laying herself down and disappearing back into her physical self. Her body gave a sudden deep breath, and her eyes opened.

"Now, Tara," she commanded. Then her eyes closed again.

I walked to my body, past Alaric, who was staring in amazement at Mayveer, and started to slip inside. But something stopped me before I could fully remerge with my body. Looking back at the opening, I saw my mother. She smiled and gave me a look of complete and utter warmth and love. She pressed her fingertips to her mouth and kissed them, then opened her hand and blew the kiss to me. What should have been silent and unseen became a stream of light that went from her fingertips to my soul. "Be at ease, Daughter. I will see you again in the Blessed Isles, where we can speak at length about the past and the future. Return to the living world now."

I cannot put into words the feeling that came over me with those words. I suddenly felt my heart beat and my lungs breathe in the air. I smelled Alaric and the mulled wine he held to my lips and tasted what seemed to be the drink of the gods to my newly awakened sense of taste. I opened my eyes and smiled up at him. I finally felt at ease with what I had done, and knew in my Anima, my soul, that I had done what was fated to be done.

"I am to have food," I whispered to him. "I think some cheese and bread would be good."

Alaric's eyes widened, but then he smiled and lifted me up a little while he piled pillows behind me. "Here is fresh cheese and bread and some mulled wine. Culluchan said you would ask for these, and I didn't believe him. I wasn't even sure you were still alive, so still were you, and you seemed not to breathe, and I felt no heartbeat."

"My spirit was journeying, so the body was empty for a bit," I told him. "Your presence here kept me safe from those Otherworld Beings who would have used this chance to take over my body. I have returned, and I will not take this journey again in This Life."

"The Master Lifenstone is gone from your hands," Culluchan remarked. "I take it your journey was successful."

"Indeed," I answered. "The Master Lifenstone is safe in the Well of Life until we have need of it again in Another Time. Now, we have but to make arrangements for the Crowns once we are gone. I know, good friend, that you will see to them."

"I will indeed," he answered. "And you must remember to put down clues as to their whereabouts before you and Alaric partake in the Final Battle. I will be there and will see the crowns safe to their place when the time comes, but it is you who must provide the clues to the Future Seeker."

"As well, I know," I answered. "I will think on this and devise some clues that will lead to the crowns while at the same time assuring that only the One who is so fated will be able to retrieve them."

So I ate and rested, as did Mayveer. Soon, we felt stronger, and we left the Realm of the Sidheran to return to Eirlandia. At least, Alaric, Culluchan and I did.

Mayveer stayed behind, saying that she was now ruler in Sidhera, and she would organize her people's part in the last battle and see to their safety and survival no matter what the outcome 'above the world,' as she put it.

So now the tale of the Master Lifenstone is done. When next I write, I shall speak of the Crowns and their fate. I do not worry about others reading this after me and somehow finding the Master Lifenstone, for the Realm of the Sidheran is secret in itself, and the Forbidden Realm is secret even from most of the Sidheran. They will be the ones to decide when to reveal the dwelling place of the Master Lifenstone and to whom.

The Master Lifenstone is no longer my concern, but I write this account so that, when the time comes, and this book is found, the steps it describes can be given to the Seeker so that the Sidheran will know the Seeker is the true Heir and will reveal to her the hiding place of the Master Lifenstone, although she will still have to brave the terrors of the Forbidden Realm.

Maeve looked up from the book, tears in her eyes. She had had no idea of the sacrifice Tara had made in concealing the Lifenstone. The story of the ArdRighian's journey left her feeling almost as if she had travelled to the Forbidden Realm. She was almost afraid to read about the Last Battle and the Ultimate Sacrifice, which ended with Tara and Alaric giving up their lives in order to keep the Crowns safe. She knew the history, certainly, but she wasn't sure she could stand reading it in the ArdRighian's own hand.

And then she thought about it. "How can the ArdRighian write what happened to the Crowns when she died protecting them?" she wondered to herself. "Is the last part of this journal the ArdRighian's writings or someone else? Is it a mixture of both, perhaps? If the ArdRighian and Consort died wearing the crowns, how would Tara know what happened to them? Are our stories of that time even accurate? Should I simply bring this back to Kilawey and let my ArdRighian Tara sort it out?" The questions ran through her head over and over, but she could come to no answer. "I've read too much to simply stop now," she finally decided. "The story is almost done. When I know the truth, I can return to ArdRighian Tara and tell her what I know, thereby sparing her the pain of reading this for herself."

The decision made, Maeve took a moment to make tea and to eat. Then, settling herself as comfortably as possible, she opened the book for what she assumed would be the last time and began to read.

I write these words with sorrow. My beloved Eirlandia is in dire trouble, and I fear she will not be in the same land for a long time. A Chapter of her history is ending, and I am but a pawn of fate in this story.

Tonight, I must use all the power I possess to create a lie. And no one must know of it except my faithful Culluchan.

Not even Alaric must suspect my duplicity, and that wounds me to my core. For the future of this land, however, the veil must be drawn over my doings so that no one can give away the secret.

In the Dark Hour, I will take the Ruling Crowns and hide them, with Culluchan's help, in a place that only the Seeker chosen by my future self will be able to re-discover. I pray I am right in believing that I will again walk the sweet lands of Eirlandia and that Alaric will once again walk at my side. For if I am wrong, I will have possibly condemned my land to eternal darkness and strife.

And when I have done this deed, I must make a mock set of crowns for us to wear in battle, and they must seem to all eyes and senses to be the real things. It is these that people will see removed from our heads by Culluchan and secreted away in yet another secret place. I would write this not at all, except Culluchan has assured me he will put this book in a place that only a special person, called by fate, would be able to find and open.

From the twinkle in his eye when he said this, I gather it will be a spot that is hidden in plain sight, for Culluchan loves to play with people's minds.

You who read these words know that the Hidden Vale is known only to the ArdRighs and ArdRighians of Eirlandia from time out of mind. No power on earth or in the underworld can be used to locate this vale, unless the Chosen One is present. To my future self, and her Chosen Seeker, I say these words, and only I will understand them.

"Seek the place where the light does shine, but once a year. Within the darkness hides the Guide, who is both terrible and powerful. To disturb the Guide is to court disaster, so tread with light steps and find the passage to the Chamber of the Ancestors. Within yourself shall you find written the Path of Salvation, and at the end of that path is the goal you seek."

Know, too, that only with the help of the Master Lifenstone will you be able to retrieve the True Crowns. Also, the False Crowns will hold within themselves other clues to the whereabouts of the True Crowns. Seek and find those first, then the Master Lifenstone, then the True Crowns. Only in this order will you succeed. The blessings of the Greater Beings upon you and upon this land and that of Vikland. I pray with all my being that, someday, Eirlandia and Vikland will again unite, this time permanently and that, together, they shall usher in a new Golden Age such as the world has never known.

I will write no more in this book. I will be too exhausted after the Workings to do more than sleep, and I know I will not survive this battle. I know that the Drui will see that the story of the Battle is recorded, and Culluchan will see to the hiding of the False Crowns and the construction of the riddle that will reveal them.

All that can be done to ensure the future of Eirlandia has or will be done before I seek the solace of the Other World and await a new life here in Eirlandia.

I wonder how this land and its people will have changed by the time I see them again. Oh, well, I shall have much to ponder in my Next Life, won't I?

My life will be counted as a short one, in terms of this mortal plane. Three tens and nine summers have I beheld, a short time for a soul to dance in the sun, some would say. But what I have seen and done is more than most, and I am content.

Farewell, all my Beloveds. I will see you again someday.

Chapter 20

Maeve

Maeve closed the book slowly, tears in her eyes. She felt satisfied that she had finished the book and somewhat angry that she knew little more now than when she had started reading days ago.

Yes, she could save the scholars time by showing them the passages that were most helpful in figuring out how to find the missing Master Lifenstone and Crowns, but she would still have nothing but this book to give to her Tara.

In the end, she felt as if she had simply wasted time on this task. Or, at least, part of her thought that. Another part still marveled at the story of the First Tara, of her courage and her skill and power.

Maeve hoped that she would be able to have the leisure to read the entire journal again someday and not skip over the years that spoke of the founding of the Eirlandian-Vikland coalition. Still, she had here and now to deal with, and the future would just have to take care of itself.

She checked the time and decided she would simply start for home in the morning instead of doing a Sending. Oh, she would Send, but only to say she was halfway home and to have someone meet her with a fresh horse so she could return all the quicker.

It was obvious from the writing that the next steps of the journey would be Tara's to make, and Maeve did not envy her mistress the task. The scholars would have to figure out where the False Crowns were hidden and retrieve them. Perhaps the ArdDrui would be helpful in that, for surely his predecessors would have passed down the knowledge of the location of the False Crown.

After the False Crowns were retrieved and their secrets revealed, Tara would have to figure out how to journey to the Forbidden Realm to retrieve the Master Lifenstone. Finally, someone would have to figure out the final clues regarding the True Crowns, journey to their hiding places, and return safely to Kilawey in time to accomplish her plan to unite Eirlandia and Vikland again before the next End of Harvest. A Full Cycle seemed both a long time and a very short time to get all this done.

Maeve packed her things to be ready to leave at first light and lay down on the bedding. Closing her eyes, she breathed a prayer to the Ancestors to watch over her and ArdRighian Tara until all could be accomplished.

Then she slipped into the Realm of Sleep and knew no more until the birds again awoke her to a new day.

The morning was bright and clear, which made Maeve smile. The weather was holding, it seemed, and she could only hope it would continue to do so until she again reached Kilawey.

Going outside, she climbed a small hill nearby and sat in the light of the rising sun. Putting herself into the light trance that accompanied a Sending, she sought out Aelfund.

"Greetings, Maeve," she heard Aelfund say in her mind. "It has been enough time that I was beginning to worry. Were you successful?"

"Moreso than we could have imagined," she answered in turn. "I have skimmed the Book of Tara and found out we need the Master Lifenstone and that there are two sets of crowns, and we need them all if the plan is to be successful."

"Another Lifenstone? Why?" asked Aelfund

"The one ArdRighian Tara has is not the Master Lifenstone," she answered. "The Master Lifenstone was sealed away in a place in Sidhera called the Forbidden Realm. ArdRighian Tara has to spirit journey back there to retrieve it. It is complicated, and I will tell you more when I come.

"Please send a runner and a fresh horse down the path to the First Way Station, and I will meet him there. He will also need to bring supplies to restock the Fourth Station for what I used."

The Sending finished, Maeve stumbled back down the hill and rested for a little bit. Sending was hard when you didn't do it often, and Maeve had never been far enough away from Kilawey before to need to use that mental discipline.

She had always been able to rely on her birds and other messengers, but the trip here had necessitated not bringing anyone or anything else along in case of traps or other things. She had even had to make the last five miles or so by foot instead of on horseback.

Much had been rumored about the old library in the Nemed at Kilawey, and almost all of it was wrong. Maeve would be telling her story many times to many different people when she returned so that records could be updated and teams of scholars sent to the library to shift through the debris to find what treasures might still lay hidden under the rubble.

About an hour later, Maeve felt strong enough to shoulder her tote and the bag containing the Book and start off toward the next Way Station, where, hopefully, a horse would be waiting to speed her return to Kilawey.

Although Aelfund had not responded to her request, Maeve knew that he would have commanded a horse and rider be sent immediately. Only if he had been unable to comply would he have Sent back to her.

She walked through a land on the edge of winter. The wind was cool, but the sun was shining. The few fields she skirted were stripped of their harvest. The New Year had just occurred, and all would be preparing for the long nights and short days of the Dark Time.

Maeve kept alert but felt no inkling of problems anywhere in her area. The road was wide and well-maintained. The Kingdom was not as wealthy or powerful as in the old Tara's day, but it was still peaceful enough in the interior, where raiders never penetrated.

Cresting a hill in midafternoon, Maeve spotted the next Waystation. This was much larger than the one she had spent the last night in. This was a permanent Fighdrui station, with a large barn for the messenger horses and other animals that the Fighdrui used in their roles as Royal Spies, Messengers, and even, sometimes, Stealth Fighters.

She could see smoke rising from the chimney, and it looked like several horses were loose in the corral adjoining the barn, not having been put into their stalls for the night yet. Anticipating a good meal and warm mead, Maeve increased her pace, planning to reach the Station before the late autumn sunset.

About two-thirds of the way there, Maeve heard the sound of a horse being ridden fast coming from her left. There was another road joining hers just ahead, and it was obvious whoever was on the horse was on that road.

Maeve hurried to the crossing, then stepped out of the road to the side, standing silent and almost invisible in the shadows of the trees around her. She felt no inkling of concern, but it was best to be safe, and if the rider was coming as fast as it seemed, they might not see her in time.

In a few moments, a rider did indeed appear, coming at a swift pace on what was obviously a Royal Steed. The rider kept looking backward as if expecting to see something, though no followers were in sight.

Nearing the crossing, the rider pulled up on the reins, slowing slightly. Maeve felt it safe to reveal herself, and stepped back into the roadway, although she stood at the very edge and away from where the horse would turn.

The effect was startling and unexpected. The rider's eyes widened, and the horse almost stopped in mid-step, rearing up in panic.

A bolt from the man's weapon went whistling by Maeve just a finger width away from striking her. Maeve stood her ground and threw back her cloak so the stranger could see the Fighdrui emblem sewn on her tunic.

She knew she wasn't well known to the outlying Fighdrui and assumed the rider had been startled enough to consider her a problem. The bolt, even if it had struck, would not have killed her, only wounded.

Controlling the horse, the rider stopped and stared hard at her momentarily. "Who are you?" he demanded harshly. "And what are you doing on that road? No one travels that path unless they have come from the Disputed Lands. You wear the Crest of the Fighdrui, but I have heard of no one of our clan being in the Disputed Lands for some time."

Maeve held her weapon hand up in peace and spread her cloak so he could see she was weaponless. "I am Maeve, Fighdrui to ArdRighian Tara herself. I have been on a confidential royal mission to the Great Library on the edge of the Disputed Lands and am now returning to Kilawey. I look forward to spending the night at the Waystation. Do you travel there also?"

The Messenger cocked his head as if listening, then looked up to where a Spy Eagle sat perched in a tree above Maeve, hidden almost completely by the foliage.

Maeve followed his gaze and chided herself for not sensing the bird's nearness. The eagle swooped down and onto the waiting arm of the Fighdrui.

"This is Lugh," he said, indicating the bird. "He tells me you speak truthfully. He also says you hold a secret in your pouch, and I am anxious to hear your tale regarding it."

Suddenly, he smiled, and his whole face changed. "I am called Talisean," he said. "I bring important news to the Council and

ArdRighian regarding the movements of the Displaced. Ride with me, for I, too, journey to the First Station for the night."

Maeve smiled back and easily mounted the horse. Talisean moved forward at a good but not speeding pace. "My news is time-sensitive," he told her, "and I have been followed part of the way here. I seem to have lost them, however. I take it you are riding to Kilawey also? We can journey together come the morrow if you wish." He smiled, turning back toward her. "I am sorry about my reaction. Things are getting tense in the outlying areas, and you startled me."

Maeve smiled back, "I understand. It was partially my fault; I should have given a sign I was there before I moved as I did." She shrugged. "I don't have a lot of field experience, and I am a little rusty."

Talisean nodded and urged the horse to a slightly faster pace. "I wish to get to the Station as soon as possible. They have been putting up barriers come nightfall, and we need to reach the limits of the Station before those are activated, or we might not get in."

Maeve was quiet; there seemed no need to reply, though she wondered what had happened to put the Fighdrui on such a high alert status. Was the situation graver than she had been led to believe? Or had things moved rapidly in her absence? She wished she could just transport herself back to Kilawey that instant. But even the most powerful Drui could not bring other than themselves such a distance, and it was the Book that was the most precious.

They traveled the rest of the way in silence. The Way Station was well provisioned and even had a Caretaker who provided food, baths, and decent beds for the two of them.

Maeve had said nothing to Talisean about the Book or her adventures, and he had not pushed. She hadn't asked about his news either, assuming that both of them needed to report to their superiors first before making any knowledge known to others, even other Fighdrui.

Maeve wasn't even sure if Talisean was a Fighdrui or something else. She assumed he was Drui of some sort since he had a Spy Bird, but one could never be sure.

The two talked about the weather, and Talisean told her that things were tense but had not erupted into fighting, at least not yet. Talisean stole some glances at her pouch but said nothing further. Maeve noted that Lugh was not with them and assumed the bird had been sent ahead to tell of their coming.

The following night was spent in the open, but the weather had actually warmed unexpectedly, and Maeve was fairly comfortable. Tomorrow would see her in Kilawey, and she was fervently wishing she could somehow wish herself into the Royal Dun right that moment. 'The sooner I can get this information to ArdRighian Tara and the Council, the more chance I have of helping find the Crowns,' she thought to herself as she settled in for the night.

She dreamt of the original Tara that night. It seemed the ArdRighian was trying to tell her something, but no words came out.

The ArdRighian kept pointing to a towering mountain that Maeve was not sure she had ever seen before. "Beneath the roots," Tara kept mouthing. "The Way lies beneath the roots."

Then the dream faded, and Maeve slept dreamless the remainder of the night. In the morning, the dream was forgotten, and Maeve was up early, saddling the horse she had received at the Station.

"I must travel as quickly as possible," she told a sleepy Talisean. "I will see you at the Nemed. Come to the Royal Enclosure when you are done with your report and ask for me. We will have a nice drink and tell each other our stories."

"But the ArdRighian needs this information, as does the ArdDrui and the council, as quickly as possible. It seems we are under a time constraint, and there is more work to be done before all can be revealed and the deeds accomplished."

As she spoke, she finished securing the bags and mounted them. "May the roads rise up to meet you, the wind be at your back, and the sun shine warm on your face," she intoned.

"May the Great Ones hold you in the palms of their hands," Talisean replied. It was the standard farewell of all Fighdrui, which told Maeve one of the things she had wondered. Talisean was truly of the Fighdrui.

"Until Kilawey, then," she said. "Until Kilawey," he answered.

Maeve turned her mount's head and headed down the path to the road, where she let the steed loose and almost flew down the road. The steed was one of the Runner Breed, who could go at a fast pace for hours without losing breath or stride. They were used mostly by messengers, but Maeve had claimed one for this last leg, knowing that speed was going to be essential.

Chapter 21

Maeve reached the Royal Nemed in almost record time, she estimated. Moving swiftly, she sent a servant to inform the Head Fighdrui, The ArdDrui, and The ArdRighian of her return.

"Tell them I will meet them after I have washed from my travels and had a small meal," she told the servant. She could tell from the boy's expression that he was startled that she would so order the ArdRighian and her advisors, but he nodded and went to do her bidding.

Maeve smiled grimly. She had more power than almost anyone in the Nemed knew about, other than those three. They would understand the reason for her delay.

She strode into her rooms, calling for a bath and stripping her clothing as she went. The satchel with the book had already been sent to the ArdRighian as soon as she entered the gates. With luck, Tara and her advisors would be poring over it, another reason she knew she had time for a few personal matters.

After a good cleaning, a small but decent meal, and the donning of fresh clothing, Maeve felt refreshed and ready to face the next part of her task. Placing the symbol of her rank around her neck, she strode through the Nemed, nodding briefly to those she passed whose rank was equal to or greater than her own.

Within a few moments, she was entering the ArdRighian's private quarters, the guards already swinging the doors shut behind her. Maeve stepped into the parlor and stopped dead.

There, sitting with Tara and in deep conference with Master Aelfund and ArdDrui Elaroth, was none other than Talisean.

Hearing the door, the four of them looked up. Tara smiled broadly. "Ah, my wonderful Maeve, welcome home. I see your mission was a great success. And I hear you have much more to tell us. Come, sit here next to me. I know you have just eaten, but would you like some mead?"

"A drink is in order, I believe," Maeve answered, still in shock from seeing Talisean. Maeve sat and accepted a goblet from Aelfund. She sipped, not taking her eyes off the man she had assumed to be a simple messenger but who was clearly more by the look of things.

"My apologies for keeping my complete identity a secret, Maeve," Talisean said after the silence began to grow awkward. Slowly, he drew back his hair from his face, and she saw the pointed ears that marked a Sidheran, although they were somewhat rounded.

"I was on a mission and had my own secrets to keep. My true nature is not known to many here and must be kept that way.

Master Aelfund took this moment to break into the story. "Young Talisean is ArdRighian Tara's half-brother, born of a Sidheran mother from a dalliance the old King had before he ever married. He was raised by the Sidheran and taught all a prince needs to know."

Maeve looked at her superior quizzically. She was having trouble believing she had never seen the young man before at some point.

Before she could ask a question, however, the ArdDrui took up the tale. "When Tara came to the throne, Talisean came here in secret, with letters and proof of his identity. He approached Tara and offered her his services as spy, messenger, and other things as needed. He has mostly been gone from the Nementon, tasked with keeping peace in the various clans, allowing Tara the time to consolidate her power as well as finding and learning to wield the power of the Master Lifenstone and the Ruling Crowns when needed."

"My good Talisean is very talented in many things and will be of great help in the next step of our plan," added Tara. "Since he lived in Sidhera for many years, he can help me get to the Forbidden Lands and find the Master Lifenstone. I have you to thank, Maeve, for finding out about that and how important it is."

"Retrieving the Master Lifenstone will be Tara and Talisean's task," chimed in Aelfund. "But your role in this is not through. As a Fighdrui, you must be the one to find the Crowns and return them to Tara. She will not be able to be gone long enough to do the rest of the hunting herself. Once she has the Master Lifenstone, you will seek out the Ruling Crowns, using the power of the Master Lifenstone to help you."

"But the Book said we must find both crowns, the false and the true," Maeve protested. "And the false crowns must be found first, then the Master Lifenstone, and then the true crowns, in that order. I remember reading that clearly."

Aelfund smiled benignly. "Do not trouble yourself over that," he told her. "The false crowns were retrieved by the Drui once it was confirmed that the girl child born to the last king was indeed the reincarnation of the original ArdRighian Tara. That is why our ArdRighian was given her name, a name no girl child in all of Eirlandia has been given since the death of the Great ArdRighian Tara Prima.

Maeve looked at her friend and ruler at this point, who shrugged. It seemed that Tara

Secunda, while apparently being the reincarnation of Tara Prima, had as yet no recollection of her past life.

"The false crowns are being examined as we speak," interrupted Elaroth, "by the best minds in the Kingdom, and soon, they will yield their secrets about the whereabouts of the Ruling Crowns. Once Tara has the Master Lifenstone and returns it here, your journey will begin."

"This will be a long and arduous journey and one that must be accomplished in as short a time as possible," continued Aelfund then, not even glancing in the ArdDrui's direction. "While you are gone searching, we will be communicating with King Alaric in secret. As soon as the Crowns are found and returned, Alaric and Tara shall marry and be crowned. We must accomplish this as quickly as possible before the rebellious Righs completely unite and possibly even find a way to bring the Formorrid in to help them."

"The Formorrid?" Maeve questioned. "I thought they were long gone."

"Unfortunately, no," answered the ArdDrui Elaroth. "Although they were severely weakened in the original Tara's time, the intervening centuries have allowed them to regain much of their strength. We are still yet unsure how this was accomplished. The Formorrid are skilled in magic, but they also have great scientific knowledge, which may include medical and genetic research advantages of which we are unaware.

Their special abilities are not as formidable in this age, but they are still a force to be reckoned with. We will need the combined might of the Vikes and the loyal Eirlandians, and possibly even help from the Sidheran, if they agree, to overcome them."

"I had no idea," Maeve murmured.

"Much has happened since you left," Tara answered. "You could not be two places at once, so do not upbraid yourself. You completed your mission in a timely manner and sent us information we would not have had even yet if you hadn't read parts of the book yourself. Your mission was successful beyond our dreams and gives us a head start on the next phase."

"Now you must rest and resume your duties as First Fighdrui to the ArdRighian," said Aelfund. "You will be acting as Regent while she goes with Talisean to the Sidheran to both retrieve the Lifenstone and, hopefully, enlist their aid in the coming conflict."

"Regent?" repeated Maeve. "I have no skills in that regard! And I have not been elected! No one will follow me!"

"On the contrary," replied Talisean, "you are well known and respected. You are actually a cousin to the ArdRighian on your father's side. The former ArdRigh was not the only one to have youthful dalliances with Sidheran women." He winked and smiled broadly. "I have no time now to go into your family history, but I promise I will tell you all about your lineage when Tara and I return with the Master Lifenstone.

"Know, though, that your appointment has been told to the High Council, and they have already confirmed your regency in this critical time period. It is not the first time in our history that a regent has been appointed, and the High Council was voted in just as Tara was, so they have the trust of the people. Master Aelfund and Second Drui Culluchan will be your chief advisors, and you will have little real power, but it will be enough to keep the wolves of war at bay while Tara and I go a-hunting."

"It seems," said Maeve slowly, "that I am but a puppet of the fates." "No," answered Elaroth gravely.

He stood and extended his staff of office over her. "I speak now the words of the Great Ones, given to me in a dream but last night. "You, Maeve of the Fighdrui, Keeper of Secrets and Lore, are not the puppet of the fates. You are the Child of Fate, the Chosen One, and in your hands will success ultimately rest.

'When you find the Root that leads into the Darkness that Brings Light, you will become the savior of your world.' So has said the Awen and the Awen is never mistaken."

Maeve only bowed her head in acknowledgment. Her adventures were far from over, it seemed, and her ultimate destiny was apparently fated to be the stuff of legends. 'I just hope the Awen is going to cooperate,' she thought to herself.

END OF BOOK 1 - Tales of Eirlandia

About the Author

Mariclaire Norton has been fascinated by ancient Celtic and Norse civilizations for decades, drawing inspiration from their myths, cultures, and forgotten histories. A lifelong lover of fantasy fiction, she has published poetry and short stories exploring these themes.

When she's not writing, Mariclaire volunteers as a certified therapeutic musician, bringing comfort through music at a local hospital. She lives with her husband of over forty years and a mischievous cat, both of whom provide endless encouragement and distraction in equal measure.